The Mirage of Freedom

Mr. Ramzi's Orchard

Manijheh and Farhad were seated at a cozy corner in an old-fashioned uptown eatery, chatting away. The place was crowded. The din of patrons at nearby tables and benches filled the air. The waiters went about serving, clad in traditional Shah Abbas-era attire. Two cups of Turkish coffee and a fresh dish of Baklava were on the couple's table.

Farhad looked distressed. His brown eyes seemed anxious. He took a few sips from his coffee. "I finally got the American visa. It seems all the trouble I went through to get to that country finally proved worthwhile."

Manijheh shook her head dejectedly. "So... you chose to leave for America after all!"

Farhad watched her elegant face and beautiful green eyes and noticed her sad expression. "You know I have to go. Your father won't consent to us getting married until I'm one of the rich and prominent. I've spent a lot of time lately on electromagnetic research. Columbia University is a major center for this type of study; I'm hoping to receive a scholarship from them."

"But you can pursue that work here too. Can't you?

Farhad picked up a piece of Baklava. Lifting it toward her mouth, he replied in a calm and reassuring tone, "America is the capital of technology. The opportunity there is limitless. It's the land where dreams and goals can be realized. Not only that, I've been waiting for this chance for a long time; I don't want to miss out. I know I can and will be successful there." He then softened his tone a little more. "You know very well how much your father values wealth and status."

After a brief pause, he seemed to have just remembered something. "I hear your father is considering Dariush, the son of Mohammad Aram the rug merchant. He has him in mind for you."

Manijheh looked visibly annoyed as she pulled her scarf farther down over her blonde hair. "So what if he does! I have no interest in that guy."

She turned her head away indignantly. Farhad continued as if he hadn't heard her. "I'm the son of your father's butler. The class gap between us is enormous. You're the daughter of Mr. Ramzi the famous industrialist who has money to burn. If you decide to go against your father's wishes you have to forego a life of comfort and luxury. You can't burn all the bridges behind you, can you?"

Manijheh looked questioningly at Farhad. "What do you mean by all this? That I should just marry Dariush?"

Focused on his thoughts and oblivious to her argument, he went on. "I'll have to work hard and task myself to provide you a good life. You've been indulged by your father; you're not used to hunger and discomfort. Poverty would be hard on you. But I'm used to it. I can go to bed hungry at night and still find sleep. I'm not fazed by material poverty as much as I am by the intellectual kind."

Manijheh was looking down, her pretty eyes filled with tears. "Well, how long will this academic trip last? How long do I need to hold off my father?" She asked despondently.

He stared into the distance. "I have no idea." He then turned to her. "Honestly, I don't know how long you'll be able to wait for me, or if you can wait for me at all."

She stared at him scornfully, shaking her head. "You know very well I'll be waiting for you."

Farhad smiled, his dark eyes twinkling with contentment. "Now I feel relieved." Finishing the rest of his coffee, he turned to Manijheh. "Let's get going. I have things to take care of for my visa."

……… …..

After leaving the restaurant, Manijheh hailed a cab and headed home while Farhad went about arranging his trip. On the way to her house, Manijheh stopped by the neighboring park and sat on a wood bench. She had plans with Farry, her friend, to meet up there.

Despite their divergent temperaments, attitudes and lifestyles, Manijheh and Farry had been friends since childhood. They attended elementary and high school together and entered college at the same time. Through these years spent at each other's side, their bond had grown stronger by the day.

Farry was self-assured and independent, the type of strong-minded woman who never allowed herself to be dominated. She always resented Manijhe's timid nature and her submissiveness toward Farhad and often tried to bring this passivity and weakness to Manijhe's attention. Yet her efforts were mostly in vain.

Manijheh was lost in frantic thoughts as she looked over the narrow sandy way leading to the bench, waiting for Farry to arrive. She felt as if she was drowning, caught between massive waves with no way to the shore. The uncertainty and anxiety had left her frustrated. Her father's stance against marrying Farhad didn't worry her much; her main concern now was Farhad finding a new love and leaving her behind. The mere thought of it shook her to the core. Farhad was her hope; her life; her entire world. The notion of being away from him or losing him drove her mad. A day without seeing or hearing him hardly seemed like living, but with him around, she soared and took flight. Her love for Farhad had turned her into a butterfly, dancing adoringly around his flame.

She remembered that horrible autumn when Farhad had been busy with exams and hadn't checked on her in a week. She had been manic, out of control, depressed and miserable. When Farhad finally came around and saw her condition, he became quite upset and persisted with questions until he figured she suspected him of having an

affair. He had kissed her gently and said, "How could I ever be interested in anyone other than you?"

Manijhe's love for Farhad was tender, profound and removed from pettiness. It was a lifelong affection that had developed through childhood and adolescence and taken over her entire existence. Her heart was akin to an ocean whose waves ebbed and flowed in accordance to his words and deeds. It was an unselfish, innocent love.

These thoughts kept running through her mind as she sat there waiting for Farry. The sun was slowly setting, disappearing into the far distance as night fell. A gentle spring breeze passed melodically through the leaves and branches, caressing her face. A strange sense of gloom was engulfing her heart. As the skies turned darker, she ruefully stared at the sunset. Suddenly she noticed Farry at the other end of the walkway, approaching breathlessly. Upon arriving, she sat on the bench beside Manijheh. "I worked too hard today. I'm really exhausted."

Manijheh was quiet. Farry caught a glimpse of her gloomy stare. "Why do your eyes look so sad? What's Farhad done again to make you so upset?"

Tears ran down Manijheh's face. "He finally got what he's been after. He has that American visa and will be gone soon."

"Well, since you're so distraught why don't you go with him?!" Farry said with a hint of anger.

"I tried hard to get a visa but it just didn't happen. He got one thanks to his academic record and background in research. I keep telling him let's get married so I can get a visa too, but he says we can't do that unless my father grants permission. I tell him it's not my father's business; we're grown adults and can make our own decisions. But he doesn't buy it. He's just too stubborn..."

Farry tried to calm her down. "Well, let him go then. He'll be back. You know he's in love with you. Get yourself together."

Manijheh looked up at Farry. "I'm annoyed at myself. This weakness and helplessness tortures me."

"He knows you love him," replied Farry in a soothing manner. "He's not worried about that." But suddenly she seemed angered by

Manijheh. "Why are you so alienated from everyone and so submissive to Farhad's wishes? Why don't you take a look around you, at those who love and care for you? Why do you keep overlooking Dariush?"

Manijheh smiled bitterly and remained silent. This helplessness of hers upset Farry who couldn't understand why she belittled herself in dealing with Farhad. Manijheh was talented and glamorous. She never displayed such vulnerability with anyone else. But when it came to Farhad, she became a doormat.

Farry put her hand on Manijheh's shoulder. "If you're so worried that he might leave and never come back, why don't you try to keep him from leaving?"

Manijheh covered her face with her hands. "I've tried so hard to convince him not to go, but his mind is made up," she replied mournfully. "I'm only demeaning myself. This fire inside him can't be doused by me or anyone else; he won't rest until he reaches his goal. It's this exact mentality that sets him apart from others and fascinates me with him."

Farry pointed to a bird flying solo high into the distance and smiled knowingly at Manijheh. They sat there for a while. It was now getting dark. Farry got up. "Let's go. I have someone to meet."

They said their goodbyes and Manijheh headed home.

....

On the way to the house, Manijheh was downhearted. Farhad's departure meant the loss of her hopes and dreams, the crumbling of the palace she had built on wishful fantasies. In her view, Farhad's reasoning was childish – "*I have to find wealth and prominence in America if I want to marry you.*" This seemed realistic and practical to Farhad, but Manijheh found it riddled with terrible complications. Adapting to a new environment; to customs and norms of another culture; to new people and new adventures and what may come from those adventures... All that aside, don't they always say, "*out of sight, out of mind*"?

Tormented by these thoughts and unsure of what to do about them, she arrived home and headed straight for Salar's room in the orchard. He was reading a book. Upon hearing her say hello, he raised his head and saw the look of despair on Manijheh's face. "What's the matter sweetheart? What happened?"

"Farhad finally did it," she answered with tears in her eyes. "He got the visa. He's really leaving."

Salar's tone was a mixture of sadness and sympathy. "This is nothing to get down about. He'll just go and come back."

Manijheh looked at him irritated. "I guess we'll see," muttered the young woman as she left the room.

....

It was late when Farhad got home. He wasn't feeling much better than Manijheh. He too was gripped with worry and concern; how could he leave her behind? He had grown up with her. They were childhood playmates. He still remembered the first time he told her he loved her; it was at Mr. Ramzi's plantation under that spruce tree. She had put her fingers to his lips and said, "*Hush, someone might hear.*" He still remembered the pleasant warmth of her fingers.

Manijheh was the daughter of Mr. Ramzi, the boss of Farhad's father, Salar Sarmad. Salar had raised Ramzi's children since they were little, and Farhad had felt the class disparity with that family from a very young age. Mr. Ramzi's children lived a life of comfort and luxury, immersed in wealth and extravagance, while he and his brother Kaveh lived with his father in the custodian's two-room housing on Mr. Ramzi's plantation. Despite the modest life Salar's income as a butler could provide for them, both Farhad and Kaveh managed to excel in academics. Farhad's astonishing aptitude in learning and understanding science was well-known to everyone around. He worked tirelessly to reach the highest levels of scientific studies and nothing seemed to deter him.

Farhad was well aware of his innate talent and had no doubts about his prospects. This gave him an extraordinary sense of confidence and never allowed him to feel inferior for being the son of a butler.

……………….

Salar Sarmad had met the Ramzi family through Ahmad's sister, whom everyone referred to as Auntie. Since the passing of his wife, Goli, Salar had a habit of visiting her grave every weekend at Behesht e Zahra. He would sit by her resting place tearfully and pour out his heart for hours. That was the one place where he could truly open up. His sons Farhad and Kaveh would often accompany him there.

Most Fridays when Salar was at Goli's grave, he would see a tall and attractive lady praying and reading the Koran at another tomb nearby. One of those Fridays when Salar had been especially upset and crying more than usual, the lady approached and sat next to him. "What's going on?" she asked gently. "Do you want these kids to die of grief with all this crying and wailing?"

Salar, noticing the stranger, looked in her direction. "What's it to you? Don't people have the right to cry over the graves of their loved ones?" He sounded somber and agitated.

"Do what you want," answered the tall lady irately. "It's your business but at least have some mercy on these kids. They can't just watch you carry on like this."

These words calmed Salar somewhat. He turned toward his sons and observed their depressed expressions. A childlike sorrow was evident on their faces. They sat there sad and teary eyed.

Witnessing this shook Salar to the core. He turned to the woman and appeared to open up to her. "I lost my wife in a car accident," he said with anguish. "There is no joy in life with her gone."

The woman replied in a soft, consoling tone, "But you now have an even bigger responsibility. Take a look at these kids; what do they possibly understand about life's injustices? These innocent children have no one other than you."

Salar and Auntie's friendship began this way, and she asked where he lived.

……………………….

A week after becoming acquainted, Auntie went to visit Salar. The address was hard to find. His home was in a poor area of Tehran. She brought with her a few food items and some toys. It took a few minutes before the door opened and Farhad appeared. She embraced him and Farhad screamed excitedly, "Dad, it's that lady!"

Salar came out and stood there speechless, as if he couldn't believe he'd ever see that towering woman standing in his home. Upon Salar's invitation, she entered the house. It was a small room with few pieces of furniture and a washed out carpet on the floor. Auntie noticed Kaveh's piercing stare; his sharp intellect was easily detectable. Sitting on a cushion at the end of the room, it was clear to her that those who lived there led an impoverished existence. She called Farhad and Kaveh over and embraced them both, showering them with kisses. Both boys were elated; they hadn't felt the maternal hugs of a woman for too long. Receiving their toys from Auntie, they started playing in a corner of the room.

Salar's voice brimmed with joy as he sat across from her. "Welcome! I never thought I'd see you in my house one day."

"I missed the kids. I thought to pay you guys a visit." She then looked around the room. "Are you comfortable here?"

"We had a good life when my wife was alive," explained Salar. "I lost my job after her death. It's life though, you have to get through it somehow and we manage to do that. Sometimes I do manual labor at people's homes to pay for the kids' expenses. But the rent for the room is paid for by my brother."

"Where is your brother?"

"Near Isfahan. He owns quite a bit of land which he uses for farming. To be honest I don't have the means to provide for these kids anymore. We might have to move in with my brother. I could work there and raise the children."

Auntie sighed. "If you find a job right here that can offer a livable income for you and the kids, would you stay?"

He smiled. "Of course I would stay. I would love for my sons to grow up in the city, to be raised in the capital and go to school here. I want to see them go to college."

She handed him a phone number. "Give me a call a week from now; I'm hoping to find you a job. Like you, I would prefer that these kids live in this city."

Salar gave her a clever look. "I've sacrificed a lot for my children's success and happiness. I'm willing to take any honorable work."

He was about to offer her dinner but she said, "Thanks, I have to go now. It's already late."

…………………..

Auntie had made up her mind. She knew her brother, Ahmad Ramzi, had grown weary of taking care of the house, orchard and three children all at the same time and needed someone to help him out.

Following the death of his cancer-stricken wife, Ahmad Ramzi had been reclusive for quite some time. That incident had been an enormous blow to his psyche. With his beloved wife gone he was lost and restless; the children were left to their own devices and his old mansion had gathered dirt and dust.

When she had the chance, Auntie would stop by and take care of the kids and do some housework but it wasn't enough. Ahmad Ramzi with his three young children and vast estate needed someone to be there full time and keep an eye on things.

The day she shared her idea with her brother, Ahmad accepted it immediately. This is how Salar Sarmad came to meet Mr. Ramzi and became a pillar of strength for that family.

In a section of Mr. Ramzi's orchard near the main residence, sat a small, two-room building for caretakers. Salar settled there along with his sons and furnished the place with his modest belongings. In one room he laid his old rug and in the other he set down two small carpets. Together with a few items Auntie brought over from Ramzi's house, he managed to create a decent dwelling for his family.

....

A few weeks had passed since Salar and his children had started living at Mr. Ramzi's estate. Salar did all the housework and took care of Ramzi's children, Farshid, Manijheh, and Soodabeh. He cooked for them and organized their clothes. He was now a parental figure to them as well, since Ramzi was completely out of sorts.

With Salar's presence, the house and orchard took on a new life. It took a week for him to clean up Mr. Ramzi's mansion. He dusted the furniture and rearranged some of them, giving the house a fresher appearance. Using his experience in gardening, he also trimmed the trees and reshaped the flowerbeds in front of the residence. He then emptied the large swimming pool from the odorous stagnant water, cleaned it up and refilled it. Both the garden and the house now looked revived.

One spring afternoon when Salar had just finished work and was walking toward his residence, Mr. Ramzi appeared on the mansion's balcony. He greeted his boss and asked how he was doing. Ramzi smiled and asked him to walk over. Salar went to the balcony and sat across from him. Mr. Ramzi enquired about his health and his sons, then said, "Salar, I notice my kids have grown very fond of you and your lads. They want to be around you at all times. I'm very happy about this."

"I haven't done much really," replied Salar cheerily. "They're just very nice and kind-hearted children."

"No. You may not know this, but you've done a great service for me and my kids," said Ramzi admiringly. "This house and garden were in ruins. The children were getting depressed. You and your sons brought joy back to our home. My children are now revitalized. I don't want to see sadness in their eyes ever again. That's why I want to ask you for a favor."

"What is your wish, sir?"

Ramzi rose from his chair and came over to Salar. "Imagine you have five children now. I can't attend to them; consider my kids as your own and look after them."

Salar stood too and faced Ramzi. "Of course I never thought of it any other way. I will raise them like my own children."

It was from this day that Manijheh, Soodabeh, and Farshid began visiting Salar's place more and more. He no longer saw them as Ramzi's children; he treated them the same as Farhad and Kaveh. Their sadness made him sad and their laugher made him smile. He loved them as much as he loved his sons.

Every night after dinner, Salar had a routine of reciting a few pages of Shahnameh. This went back to years ago when he would accompany his father to a local traditional gymnasium and they would perform for the athletes. At this point he knew most of the book's epic stories by heart. Salar's narrations had become a favorite habit for the children. Encouraged by their strong interest, he would describe those stories in plain words as well, recounting the honor and bravery of ancient Iranian heroes. To instill character in the children, he would also preach about the heroes' humanity and altruism and praise their assistance to the poor and downtrodden.

Salar's goal was to impart to the kids the same principles of compassion and ethics he had learned throughout his life. He tried to make sure that his sons and Ramzi's children learn the meaning of honor and integrity. He spoke to them of spiritual enlightenment and taught them that what matters in life is not wealth and status, but rather dedication to morality and faith and assistance to others.

....

The children spent their childhood together and grew up. But Farhad and Manijheh were a different story; they were two souls united as one. He never let her out of his sight and always looked out for her. Her slightest distress drove him crazy. They knew they loved each other from very early on. Even Salar had noticed their bond. Farhad would help Manijheh with her studies and sometimes even did her homework for her. But Soodabeh needed his help much less; she could take care of her problems on her own. Wise and collected, she was a pretty girl with two dimples on her cheeks that made her even cuter when she smiled. Her dark, shapely eyes had an air of mystery and she would always tie her jet black hair in the back, shaped like a beautiful flower.

High school was now over and each of the kids chose a different path for their lives. Kaveh was admitted to the agriculture university and ended up moving to Isfahan, settling on his uncle's farm. He had a crooked back and a limp in one leg. His face was not handsome but had a distinct magnetism that impressed the beholder, and he had a piercing gaze which his father likened to a meteor passing through one's soul.

As for the others, Manijheh majored in literature and Soodabeh chose architecture. Farhad was accepted into an engineering program, but Farshid abandoned academics after high school.

.. ..

Farhad aced the entrance exam for engineering. He knew why he had chosen this field and what he aimed to do in the future. He was an astute and bright young man who attracted a great deal of attention with his intellect and wisdom, and had a strikingly attractive face that drew women to him. The day the test scores were announced he was beside himself with excitement. The first person he called to deliver the good news was Manijheh. He then got himself home quickly to announce his success to his father and brother.

Salar, overcome with joy by his son's accomplishment, embraced him. "I wish your mother was here to see this. She always wanted you to attain higher education. I'll never forget her last request: *'Make sure the kids go to college.'* Her voice still rings in my ear."

After dinner, Salar told the boys, "Before I start my recitation, I want to share something with you both since we're all here. Of course it has to do with Farhad."

Farhad stared at his father. Salar continued. "My dear Farhad, I'll never forget this night for the rest of my life. I don't know how many more years I have to live, but this is one of the best nights of my entire existence. Now that I see you both grown up and in university, my mind is finally at ease; you'll be able to make ends meet even when I'm gone."

Kaveh and Farhad looked at one another puzzled and shook their heads.

Salar told Farhad, "You know Kaveh has decided to move to Isfahan and work on your uncle's farm while going to university. But what I want to talk about is related to you. I think it would be best if you left Ramzi's house as well."

Farhad was smiling but seemed surprised. "Has something happened, dad?"

"Not yet," replied Salar. "But I know something will. Everyone knows you and Manijheh have feelings for each other. You also know Ramzi's personality. I'm afraid he'll say or do something that will injure your pride, and god forbid, your studies and your future might be affected as a result. I know you have a great goal that you plan to pursue abroad. You can't achieve your dreams living in Ramzi's house."

Farhad had his head down. His eyes were fixated on the flower pattern on the old rug that was so worn it looked on the verge of disintegration. His heart started fluttering. This house, this orchard, Manijheh and all those memories ... how was he going to leave them all behind? He could still hear the sounds of their childhood games, their talks during courtship and Manijheh's lovely laughter echoing through the trees of Ramzi's garden. Often during the week they would sit together under that single tree at the end of the lot - the one they had carved a heart into - and would look into each other's eyes and chat for hours. How can anyone just abandon all that and take off?

Salar took Farhad by the hand. "I know it's hard. Leaving is always hard. But sometimes staying destroys the soul. You have a fierce heart, a willpower that will help you reach whatever you desire. It's strong enough to overcome any obstacle."

Farhad's respect for his father was immense. He kissed him on the cheek and said with a lump in his throat, "Ok father. I'll go."

………………

Hearing the news of Farhad's departure made Ramzi extremely happy. "Salar did a good thing by getting Farhad away from this house;" he told Auntie who was over for a visit, adding sarcastically, "Fire and cotton should never be next to each other."

Auntie knew her brother was aware of Manijheh and Farhad's romance and that he was happy to see Farhad go away. Not wishing to leave his sarcasm unanswered, she replied with a meaningful smile, "When a woman loves someone, the biggest obstacle couldn't stand in her way let alone her parents."

Mr. Ramzi, who rarely spoke harshly to his sister, could not restrain himself and stood up. "Sister, are you with me or are you with…"

She laughed, knowing her words had upset her brother. "I'd never want to see you hurt. You're my flesh and blood," she said gently.

She then got up to take care of a few chores around the house.

....

Ahmad Ramzi owned an aluminum-dish factory. His father had been a carpet merchant who amassed a great wealth. After the death of his father, Ramzi managed to grow that wealth multifold by investing in the manufacturing industry and went on to purchase an impressive mansion in the north of Tehran. The central building was located at the heart of a plantation enclosing large trees of pine, magnolia and willow, with bushes of acacia flowers decorating its high walls. The main residence was stylish and luxurious with a dazzling interior. The crescent windows facing the pool lent the garden an air of grandiosity and splendor that would astound any observer. The enormous living room carpeted with exquisite Persian rugs, the expensive antique furniture and the framed paintings on the walls were all indicative of the homeowner's extravagant wealth.

Ramzi had an arrogant pride about his wealth and associated only with those he perceived as equals. He had quite a few connections in government institutions whom he could call on when in a bind. But one unique trait about him was his generosity toward his children and relatives, a factor that had endeared him to the clan. He had great hopes and dreams for his children and nothing short of a quality Western education was considered adequate for them. It was for this reason that he couldn't fathom the idea of his daughter marrying someone from a much lower class than their own. Ramzi liked and respected Farhad for his continued academic achievements, but his feelings never went beyond that. Salar Sarmad knew this well, and it was for this reason that he asked Farhad to leave that house.

....

Two weeks after receiving his visa, Farhad set up a date with Manijheh to tell her the date of his departure, but also because hadn't seen her for a few days and missed her. On a breezy summer afternoon, he arrived early at the park where they were supposed to meet. He sat on a wood bench facing the pool and watched the waterworks. Narrow threads of water would shoot up slowly and then return quickly back to the surface. It reminded him of the lives of those who chase after wealth and prestige without bothering to educate themselves and end up failing due to lacking the basic foundation. But he had decided to make his way to America, the land of dreams, and pursue his education to the highest level so that he could return one day and tell Mr. Ramzi to his face: *"Now I'm actually above you."*

The park was packed. A group of people exercised on the less crowded sidewalk. The scent of Roses, Jasmines and Wallflowers planted around the pool filled the air. A pack of white pigeons dove down toward the seeds people had thrown for them. The sound of evening prayer could now be heard all over the park. Being highly spiritual, at that moment Farhad felt he was flying through the clouds; he felt close to God. For a few minutes it was as if he had left earth, its people and their petty concerns behind and was soaring through the hidden corners of creation. What a fantastic state it was. He wanted to build a home among the clouds and stay there for eternity. But suddenly the sound of Manijheh saying hello removed him from it all. She sat next to him. It had been a few days since they last saw each other. The closer it came to leaving, the more he realized how hard it was to be away from her. Manijheh asked how he was doing, but he simply looked at her. "How come you're so late?" he remarked.

"I was buying you a going-away gift."

"A gift for me?" he asked with a wide grin. "What did you get?"

"A book of Hafez poetry," she replied while removing a gift-wrapped package from her purse. "So that you can read it every day and be reminded you need to love me more."

Farhad held Manijheh's hand and placed it on his heart. "Ask my heart about my love for you. Don't wait for Hafez."

They both laughed. "This is the second book I've received as a gift today," he said as he took the book from Manijheh.

Surprised, Manijheh asked with a curious tone, "Who did you get the other one from?"

"Your father. I went to say goodbye today. He gave me a book on ancient Iranian arts. I was really happy at first. But when I opened the package, I felt as if he had slapped me in the face. You know what was in there? A million-toman check."

Farhad reached in his pocket and took out an envelope, handed it to Manijheh and said, "Tell your father I loved his gift but I can't accept his money."

She was bewildered. "Did it offend you?"

He held her hands and squeezed them. "If I was Dariush Aram, would your father still have given me a million-toman check?" he asked softly. "Now do you understand why?"

Manijheh now seemed angry. "Did you want to meet me just to talk about this stuff?"

"No," he replied gently. "I wanted to see you so I could tell you my flight date and also have dinner."

"Where?" she asked, taken by surprise.

"Anywhere you want."

"At your house," she said immediately. "I want to cook for you what you like."

Farhad could only take Manijheh by the hand and help her up.

An hour later they were in Farhad's apartment. It was a compact suite with only a few pieces of furniture and a two-person couch behind a small table. A photo of Manijheh could be seen on a desk. Farhad placed their take-out food on the table and went to the kitchen to get plates and utensils. In the meantime, Manijheh removed her scarf and overcoat and stood in front of the mirror. Doing a quick turn, she looked herself over and smiled, feeling content about her good looks. Her blonde hair was pulled back; an emerald necklace around her petite neck made it appear even more sensuous. She had an alluring dress on that ignited the flames of lust in Farhad. She looked more beautiful than ever. Turning toward the kitchen, she saw Farhad standing there watching. Yearning and desire rushed the blood to her face and set her heart racing. She approached him seductively. Every fiber of her being was drawn to him. At this moment, all her notions of self-control, guilt and restraint had lost meaning. She was reminded of this poem she'd read once in a book:

What has love to do with faith and blasphemy

What do lovers care about the soul or the body

At Farhad's direction, they sat on the couch close to each other. Manijheh placed her hands on his and asked with misty eyes, "When is your flight?" Farhad glanced at her sad, sweet face and said softly, "A few weeks from now." Feeling as if a blade had sliced through her heart, she asked dejectedly, "You're really happy to be leaving, aren't you?"

"Believe me, I won't come back empty handed," said Farhad, looking her intently in the eyes. "The lofty heights I'm aiming for have you standing at the peak."

Out of the blue, he wrapped his arms around her waist and whispered in her ear, "My precious, you're the reason I'm leaving. I'm going to return with a professional degree; so I can get rich; so I can have you."

Manijheh shot him a look. "You'll go and forget about me. I know it. You'll go…"

Farhad didn't let her finish the sentence. He pulled her close and kissed her mouth over and over. Love and desire had set him ablaze. This was a night of passion. Merged together in love and sin, they lost track of time. Farhad felt the scent of Manijheh's body for the first time and when they came back to their senses, there was nothing left standing between them. That night and those that followed were spent in each other's arms.

From then on, Farhad and Manijheh spent most days and nights together. She would often concoct excuses for her father so she could stay with Farhad overnight. She wanted to spend these last two weeks with him.

They wandered around Tehran during the day. Like two birds in love, blissful and carefree, they would head for the green countryside around the city. They dined together and walked the city parks. All others to them were invisible, as if the whole city belonged to the two of them. The world ceased to exist outside of their bond. Free of worries or concerns, they were so immersed in their own world that even lightning couldn't jolt them. How great it would have been if the world could just pause at that moment, and time could stand still.

But it didn't. The days flew by and Farhad's date of departure was now here. They were both amazed by the quick passage of time. It felt as if it was only yesterday that they had consummated their love, promised the world to each other and shared glorious visions of their future together.

....

A few days before his trip, Farhad visited his father. Salar had just returned home exhausted from his daily chores. A cup of tea before him, he was flicking through the day's paper. Farhad stood by the open door. Salar didn't notice his presence. His son took a moment and looked around the room. This small dwelling was teeming with childhood memories. He thought about the past, to the days when Salar was young and still strong enough to pick him and his brother up; when Mr. Ramzi was still a kind man; when the plantation was so large that he, Kaveh and Ramzi's children could spend hours running among its trees; to those summer days when he and Manijheh would flirt under that pine tree and he would whisper in her ear: "*We should never be apart.*"

He was nudged out of these daydreams by his father's voice. "Hello."

Farhad, as if awakened from sleep, was silent for a moment, then hurried to his father's side. Salar happily offered him a seat. He complied and said, "I came to tell you what day I'm leaving." "Thank God," answered Salar, aware of Farhad's plans. "It was always your mother's wish for you to see the world and get a good education." He then reached under his cushion and grabbed a booklet for his son. Farhad looked at it. "What is this?"

"That's my checkbook. It's for the money I've saved for your trip."

"But you know I already have enough," said Farhad, gratefully. "Use this money to buy yourself a house and leave this place. How long do you want to keep working? What will people think? You have two educated sons; won't people wonder why you're still a servant here?"

"I don't live for other people," said Salar. "Why should I care what they think? I've never been a follower. Besides, Kaveh bought me a house in Tehran just a year ago... What am I to do? With Farshid still needing guidance and coming home bloodied and bruised all the time, someone has to be here for him."

He paused for a second. With Farhad listening in amazement, he added, "You should have seen how battered he was last week! He had blood all over his face and could barely make it to my room. You know why? He'd been drunk again and got himself beaten up. He was too afraid to even leave his room for three days. His father is too busy dreaming of wealth and prestige. What would be the point of me leaving in the middle of all this? You know how I much hate freeloading and uselessness. I understand the meaning of life; I know how short it is. I know a person's legacy is far more important than the nonsense imagined by petty and superficial folks."

Farhad observed his father's worn and weathered hands and felt a deep sense of sadness; he knew those hands well. He raised his head, looked in his father's gentle eyes and thought, "Why am I leaving his side? Where can I find another shoulder like this to lay my head on?"

But he quickly composed and reminded himself: He was leaving to climb the highest peaks of knowledge. He had too many goals. His willpower was too strong to be shaken even by his feelings for Manijheh.

From a very early age, Farhad had an intense curiosity about the properties of objects and everything he saw around him. He pondered the effects of those objects on the lives of humans and their relationships with each other. He had always wondered about the secrets that could be behind their creation. Now, he wanted to find the answers.

When he entered college, he majored in physics and specialized in electromagnetics. Sometimes he would be so preoccupied with numbers that he'd lose touch with the outside world. He had a tremendous respect for inventors and scholars such as Alan Turing, one of the pioneers of computer technology. He knew that electromagnetic forces encompassed the universe and it's through them that humans may understand some of the marvels of creation.

This handsome, educated and well-respected young man had a fascination with the type of natural phenomena whose mysteries seemed hard and even impossible to solve.

·········

The Starry Nights at the Farm

In Ahmad Ramzi's family, Soodabeh was a unique character. If people didn't know her as Ramzi's daughter they might have even assumed her father was someone else. She may have lacked Manijheh's alluring beauty, but had a certain poise and elegance that attracted the observer. Tall and slender, her figure always drew compliments especially when dressed in dark gowns. She was an independent thinker and always stood by her words and decisions. Auntie and Salar had a special respect for her; when faced with a problem and in need of advice they usually sought her out. She was a confidant for everyone she knew, keeping secrets of others deep in her heart. But this kind and trustworthy being had a secret of her own that she could not share with anyone. In her heart, a special place was reserved for Farhad. Like Manijheh, she too had grown up with him and considered him an exceptional person. She often felt that nothing made her happier than being around him. She wanted to see him every day, talk to him and enjoy his companionship. She wished just once she could close her eyes and tell Farhad she loved him, but alas, it was clear he was head over heels for Manijheh. This made her decide to forget about her feelings for Farhad and to simply keep that sentiment as a cherished souvenir for her own heart. She told herself that this is only a natural attachment that will disappear over time. Soodabeh was a success in her profession. She traveled extensively due to her job, and sometimes when she was in Isfahan, she would visit her old playmate Kaveh on his vast farm.

Exactly a week before Farhad's departure, Kaveh phoned Soodabeh, saying he needed help with his idea for building a township. He wanted her to draw up and execute the plans. She accepted the offer, knowing this would help her feel less depressed about Farhad being gone.

....

Kaveh stood on the balcony of his two-room rural home, looking over the farm. It was one of those hot summer mornings in Isfahan, but the mild wind made the heat more tolerable. His assistant, Moosa, attended to the two horses recently purchased.

"This one is a purebred," shouted Moosa upon seeing Kaveh. "I've named it Saani. It'll be a good horse if I can train it well. That other one is lazy though. I hope it's not sick."

Kaveh walked over to the horses. He stroked the mane of the one Moosa called lazy. "It's not all that bad. Could end up pretty good if we attend to it. I'll look after this one myself."

"You sure love to take the damaged and downtrodden under your wing," said Moosa, jokingly. Kaveh looked around the farm with a faint smile. "The weather is nice." Pointing to a far region of the farm, he added, "I'm going to plow that part."

"Should I bring the tractor?"

"No, I'll get it myself," said Kaveh as he walked over to it.

A few steps farther ahead, he turned to Moosa. "Tell Abdol not to take the sheep near the cattle house. The agriculture department is coming to inspect that place today. I don't want any unforeseen problems."

Moosa laughed. "Abdol is at his fiancé's house, sir. They're going shopping for the wedding."

"Way to tell people!" said Kaveh sarcastically, feeling he should have known about this. "At least he could have had us ornament this tractor for him; how's he supposed to get around with that sputtering motorbike? Alright then, tell Kamal to come instead."

Then without waiting for Moosa's answer, he limped toward the tractor, got himself behind the wheel and turned it on. He drove back and forth a bit. He'd just gotten the thing back from the shop. Minutes later, dirt and dust went up in the area he was plowing. He planned to grow corn there.

....

Around noon when it got hot, Kaveh quit working. He parked the tractor and headed to the house. His right leg was bothering him. Last year when his back was operated on, he had asked the doctor about his leg and was told it couldn't be helped until his back was fixed. He had learned to put up with the discomfort and always told himself that one day the leg will get better. At least now he could walk straight; the hump on his back was only noticeable from the side. Kaveh was tall and built. His masculine demeanor had a certain charm. People who heard his voice without seeing him would mistake him for Salar. He had been on this farm for years, living in that two-room house. He liked the peace and quiet here. He had furnished one of the rooms with a desk, a few chairs and a computer, and turned it into an office. All the workers knew the room wasn't to be entered when he was busy studying or attending to the farm's business. A large bookshelf full of books sat in the corner of the office. In the other room, a beautiful carpet made in Isfahan was laid down and surrounded by cushion seats. This is where he would dine and socialize with the farm workers and also host his guests.

The phone rang as he was about to enter. Picking up, he heard Moosa who had just remembered to tell him about the dinner party at his uncle's house.

"Uncle knows I'm not the party type," said Kaveh in response. "Besides, Soodabeh is coming from Tehran today."

"When will MS. Soodabeh get here?" asked Moosa. "What are we going to do about dinner?"

"Four in the afternoon," answered Kaveh. "But my good man, we haven't eaten lunch yet and you're already worried about dinner. Hurry over; I'm cooking some proper food."

He then hung up.

Kaveh entered the kitchen. He turned on the stove, put the skillet on top and poured some corn oil in it. As he was breaking and adding the eggs, he noticed one of them was a double-yolk. He thought to himself, 'And there's Soodabeh's arrival. She's always a good omen.'

He set down the plates and went to get the warmed up food and bread. Moosa and Abdol's brother, Kamal, had now arrived. At Kaveh's invitation they sat down for lunch. While everyone was eating, he turned to Kamal. "Your brother's not into work anymore. He won't calm down till he gets married."

Kamal chuckled and answered politely, "You'll have to forgive him, sir. It's close to his wedding. He's getting married for the first time."

Kaveh laughed out loud. "How many more times is he planning on getting married?"

He then gestured to Moosa to pass him the water jug.

Moosa poured some water for Kaveh, and as if something had just occurred to him, asked, "Sir, you have no extra rooms here. Where will Ms. Soodabeh sleep then?"

Kaveh put his glass down on the floor spread. "First of all, this place has two rooms. Second, I don't think Soodabeh is staying here. I'll send her to my uncle's house. It'll work out even better since they already have guests."

"You know, you never talk about the Ramzi family," said Moosa, seeming nosy. "It seems like you don't have too many good memories from them."

Kaveh frowned. "I may not talk about them but they're on my mind day and night."

Moosa who had developed a friendship with Kaveh through working for him, said mischievously, "Could it be..."

Kaveh shot him a look. Moosa stopped himself and resumed eating. Kamal, who had been quiet up to that point, addressed Kaveh. "By the way, Mr. Kaveh, why do you live on this farm? With your wealth and money, why don't you go to the city? In fact why won't you get married?"

Kaveh had always allowed his workers to speak to him casually. Hearing this made him turn to Moosa and ask, "When did this Mr. Kamal of yours get so chatty? Most of the time he's too shy to even talk about basic stuff."

"Sir, I swear I wasn't being nosy," said Kamal embarrassedly, thinking he had offended Kaveh. "I just wanted to..."

Kaveh interrupted him. "Not being nosy at all. I've told you all we're friends, and now we're breaking bread together. You have every right to know about me and my life. Now that you've brought back some of my memories, let me tell you all a little about my past."

He chugged a glass of water and went on. "Look Mr. Kamal, I love the farm life. Isn't this a home by itself? So much beauty and God's blessings can be found here. You see that mountain? That's one of the walls of my house. And this expansive land, rich with wheat and plants is a luxury carpet under my feet."

He then pointed to his office room and added, "And if I ever feel like it, I can use that computer to communicate with the entire world any time of day or night. The hustle and bustle of the city does not please me. Despite my love for my father, I had to escape the chaos of Tehran. I wouldn't trade the peace and quiet on this farm with anything."

Moosa took the opportunity and asked curiously, "Sir, why don't you bring your father here?"

Kaveh kept quiet, as if searching for an answer, and then said, "My father is a unique man. He believes in things that others may find silly. After my mother's death, we were all in bad shape both emotionally and financially. Mr. Ramzi took us under his wing; let us stay at his house; gave my father a job, and paid for me and my brother to get an education. That's why my father won't leave Mr. Ramzi to come here. When he feels indebted to someone, he'll serve them to the last day of his life."

Moosa and Kamal were all ears. "Sir, how did your mother pass away?" asked Kamal.

Kaveh's face contorted. "In a car accident on our way to Tehran from the village." He was now fighting back tears. "My mother forced my dad to move us to Tehran, because she wanted me and my brother to get an education there. I wish we'd never left and she was still alive; but it's life. Nothing we can do."

Moosa, sensing Kaveh's immense pain and hoping to change the mood of the conversation, said playfully, "So your father is another villager like us! We peasants would do anything to make others happy."

Kaveh patted Moosa's shoulder. "Of course Moosa. We're all peasants. My father was born and raised in a rural home. It was back in the feudal times when landowners treated peasants as slaves. My paternal grandfather was a savvy man. He grew rice on a piece of his family land, and to appease the village lord, every year he bribed him with some of that rice. He later married my grandmother. The products of this marriage were my father, Salar, my uncle, and my aunt Golrokh. He was a dictator in every sense of the term. He would beat my grandmother often and even forbade his sons from getting educated. But my father stubbornly put himself through school. Even though the school was in the next village, he would walk there, sometimes barefoot in the rain and snow. My father's Shahnameh narrations started around that time and continue to this day. Of course my grandparents' marriage didn't last long. Apparently one day my grandfather comes to the house accompanied by a young woman, and faced with the stunned looks of his wife and children, he tells them, 'This is Maryam, she's my new wife.' The both of them then head to another room together. Grandmother at this point loses control and lunges toward her husband. Caught off-guard at first, he starts to beat my grandmother with a stick. The kids jump in the fray to protect their mother, but he refuses to stop. Finally my father attacks him and they start grappling. Despite his small size, my father manages to push him away from my grandmother. But with extreme cruelty, my grandfather strikes my father's leg with the stick and does extensive damage, which due to lack of access to medical care, became permanent and my father has walked with a limp ever since."

Kamal and Moosa were listening attentively. They had never heard Kaveh open up about his life. "Sir, your poor grandmother must have gone through hell her entire life," said Kamal sympathetically.

Kaveh tightened his lips. "No, the pain ended soon," he answered. "Her father was a tough, athletic man. When he found out about this debacle through my father, he came to their house and took my grandmother and the children to his own home. He also sent a message to my grandfather that unless he agrees to a divorce and giving up custody of the kids, he would kill him with his bare hands. My grandfather knew what this message meant. He divorced my grandmother, Marzieh, and left the kids alone too. Grandmother took up residence in her father's house, and he took care of them and sent the kids to school. As adults, my aunt Golrokh married one of the boys in the extended family, my uncle pursed farming, and my father went into business and trade. He always says he owes all his insight and humanity to his mother's father."

Kaveh's throat felt dry now. He took a sip of water. "My father, Salar, stayed in school till the ninth grade but then had to drop out and find employment. Later he married my mother, Goli, and the products of that marriage are me and Farhad."

He then emphasized proudly, "Although my father couldn't finish school, I can assure you he's more knowledgeable and wise than most educated people."

At this point Moosa said, "Mr. Kaveh, it's clear from your accounts that your father loved his wife very much."

"Yeah, my father worshiped his wife," replied Kaveh, pensively. "In our house my mother's word was paramount. He provided us a decent life. Apparently when I was born with a physical defect, he didn't show an ounce of displeasure and even took my mother on a trip to Mashhad to take her mind off of it. When I was older and started noticing my damaged leg, he always complimented my good qualities and intelligence to make me less concerned about my disability."

Moosa, with his trademark playfulness interrupted Kaveh. "Sir, between us, your leg may be defective but in exchange God has blessed you with qualities that endear you to everyone."

Kaveh laughed out loud. "My father says the same thing. On the other hand, Farhad is handsome. When we were kids, everyone told my mother to protect him from evil eyes. Of course then the move to Tehran came up and that godforsaken accident..."He sighed and grew quiet. But he soon composed himself. "Well, you guys sure made me talk and I lost track of food and everything else. Let's get going and take care of business."

All three had a good laugh. Moosa packed away the dishes and they headed out to the farm. As they were leaving the room, Kaveh called Kamal over and handed him a check from his pocket. "Give this to Abdol. It's his wedding gift."

Kamal took the check and looked at it, then seeming to panic, held it toward Kaveh. "Sir I think there's a mistake. This is too much money."

Kaveh pushed the check back toward him and smiled. "No, I didn't make a mistake. That poor guy has a lot of expenses ahead of him."

Kamal put the check in his pocket and walked away, but said in a voice loud enough for Kaveh to hear, "I wish I was the one getting married!"

"Who's going to give you their daughter!" shouted back Kaveh. "Go handle your business."

....

The last rays of the sun were beaming over the farm when Soodabeh arrived. Hearing the car's brakes, Kaveh left his computer and rushed to greet Soodabeh as she tried to climb the stairs with a heavy suitcase. He took it from her and they went inside after exchanging pleasantries. Noticing changes in the house, she said, "The house looks a little different since last time."

Kaveh placed the suitcase on the floor and walked toward the window. "Yeah, I did a few things. I added a small bathroom to the building, widened the kitchen and changed up the decoration a little too."

Soodabeh smiled. "Is there something going on I don't know about?" she said teasingly. "Come sit by the Samovar like the old days and we'll have some tea," he replied laughing. Just like the past when she would sit there and prepare tea for everyone, Soodabeh poured some tea for herself and Kaveh.

Kaveh was eyeing her secretly. He took the cup from her and took a sip, then nodded. "The scent of your tea is just like it was back in the day in that little room on Ramzi's plantation. It smells like your hands did back then."

Soodabeh laughed. "You're still sentimental like you used to be." She then added, "You really have it good living so close to all this natural beauty. It's so calm and peaceful."

"You too could be here and live on this magnificent landscape," he said. "Why are you stuck in the city?"

"You think this damned job gives me a chance?" replied Soodabeh, opening her bag. "I have to run around all day." She then took out a few folders and files and started to sort through them.

"What's the news over there?" asked Kaveh. "Everyone ok? Tell me what's going on."

Soodabeh began placing the folders back in her bag. "Everyone's fine." After a brief pause she added, "Farhad is leaving for America. He got the visa."

"This is old news," said Kaveh. "He had this in mind for years, now his wish is finally coming true. Why are you concerned though?"

Soodabeh looked at him. "But what about Manijheh?"

"Well your father is against their marriage; Farhad has to do something to change his mind." He then stood over Soodabeh. "I asked you why you're worried."

Soodabeh blushed. He noticed it but didn't let on. "Let's go, I want to show you the land I'm planning to use for town building."

On the way, Soodabeh noticed the horses frolicking in a corner of the farm. "You ride horses too."

"I'm a good horse rider," replied Kaveh while watching the horses. Soodabeh glanced at the hunch on his back. Kaveh caught her eyes. "Don't worry. It doesn't hurt."

Back in childhood, Soodabeh always felt bad about Kaveh's hunched back and Kaveh would usually laugh it off and say, 'It doesn't hurt.' Soodabeh laughed out loud. "You always catch me."

Kaveh pointed Soodabeh to the narrow ridge leading from the center of the farm to the plot of land. Engaged in conversation, they walked the ridge. It took nearly two hours for Soodabeh to examine the plot, filming various spots and taking photos from different angles. Once the mapping was completed around dusk, they headed back home.

It was dark now. Both were tired. On the porch there was a small round table with four small chairs. A pitcher of water and a bowl of sherbet could be seen on the table. It was obvious Moosa had prepared them. Kaveh leaned back on one of the chairs. Soodabeh said she'll go inside to organize her tools. Kaveh poured himself a glass of sherbet and drank it, then filled Soodabeh's glass as well. She returned minutes later, wearing a colorful overcoat. She sat in the chair facing Kaveh. He pointed to the sherbet glass. Soodabeh picked it up briefly but put it down again. "It's night and it's getting cold on the farm so I put on an overcoat. I'll drink the sherbet later."

She shifted in her seat and pointed toward the skies. "Look at the sky, it's filled with stars. What a stunning moonlight. It's as if someone creative has lit up the whole sky."

Kaveh simply kept observing. A mild breeze was blowing. Moths flashing bright lights danced before their eyes. Nature's majesty and splendor was incomparable. Soodabeh locked eyes on him. "It's been so long since we last sat together and gazed the stars," she said. "I miss those summer nights at my father's orchard."

Kaveh pointed to a far corner in the sky. "Look at all those stars gathered in one place. That's the Milky Way."

"I know where it is," she replied with a childlike smile. "You taught me yourself."

Kaveh gently placed his hand on Soodabeh's and pressed it. But her mind seemed elsewhere. She whispered, "I don't know why Farhad needs to move to America for wealth and prestige. You didn't go there; you still managed to become rich. You still have an excellent education. A person can have it all no matter where he lives. He just has to set his mind to it."

"Maybe there are unique opportunities in America to help Farhad reach his goals," replied Kaveh. "Besides, everyone has their own way of thinking. Life can be seen from countless different angles. I stayed here and chose a life on the farm because I love nature. This soil, the wind and the rain get me closer to God. I adore the way the wind blows through the wheat fields. Every morning here I kneel down and kiss the earth. After all isn't it true that we all come from the earth and return to it eventually? As Khayyam attests:

> *In childhood we strove to go to school,*
> *Our turn to teach, joyous as a rule*
> *The end of the story is sad and cruel*
> *From dust we came, and gone with*

winds cool." (1)

Then as he kept his gaze at the far corners of the sky, he grew quiet. A few moments passed. Soodabeh, still listening intently, noted Kaveh's silence. She turned to him. She sensed he was in a state of rapture. His face at that instant was remarkably attractive. After a short while he broke the silence. "I've been thinking... is the creation of the universe a result of that trigger or so called Big Bang, which organized the galaxy through electromagnetic forces and placed this very planet which in that context is smaller than a dot in a distance from the sun just suitable enough to create life? Is this planet, this very earth we touch, dependent on that same trigger? And isn't the entire creation designed with the purpose of leading humanity to discover itself? To admire its creator and to understand the intent behind creation? To recognize the mission bestowed upon itself in this temporary dwelling? Well, to solve this great enigma I have no need to visit America."

Soodabeh's eyes were fixed on Kaveh. His words had stirred her inside. She sank deep in thought.

Kaveh, after a brief pause, returned to the topic of Farhad. "I think Farhad has a great interest in these issues as well. But he wants to arrive at the answer through scientific understanding. His motivation is so strong it leads him toward research, exploration and solving the mystery of creation. He too seeks to find himself, to discover his essence. The difference is I am an idealist and he's a realist."

Soodabeh, while intensely curious and amazed by Kaveh's inner passion, asked calmly, "But what about love? What is love's function in the middle of all this?"

"Bravo!" replied Kaveh, enthused by her question. "Love is that entity that binds everything together. Love is the manifestation of creation. That exact thing that unites humanity with its creator. As Molana proclaims:

> *Why think thus O men of piety*
> *I have returned to sobriety*

Neither flesh of dust, nor wind inspire
Nor water in veins, nor made of fire

My place is the no-place
My image is without face

I eliminated duality with joyous laughter
Saw the unity of here and the hereafter
Unity is what I sing, unity is what I speak
Unity is what I know, unity is what I
seek" (2)

Soodabeh was silent. She felt a sense of serenity she hadn't known before. Gazing upon the starry sky, her thoughts took flight. She didn't want this bliss to end. She didn't want to be separate from Kaveh. With him she felt empowered. His calm and attractive demeanor warmed her heart. Like a sturdy mountain, Kaveh was dependable, someone to lean on. She wanted to stay there next to him. Yet she knew she had to leave. Doubt and uncertainty had overshadowed her yearnings and desires. Her thoughts had grown chaotic, the misgivings made her apprehensive. She sat up abruptly and called out to Kaveh, "I have to leave. It's late."

Kaveh stared at her in disbelief. Then he seemed to remember Soodabeh's stubborn nature; that she does as she says. He stood facing her. He held her hands. "Maybe you're worried about not sleeping well here. I've arranged with my uncle for you to spend the night at their house."

Soodabeh pulled her hands away. "If I wanted to stay in Isfahan, I would have stayed right here in the farm, slept in the balcony and counted stars till dawn."

"I know you," said Kaveh. "When you say you have to go, you go. But I wish you would stay so we could count the stars together."

She patted him on the shoulder. "Well, maybe some other night. Who knows."

. . . .

With Soodabeh gone, Kaveh remained on the balcony, immersed in thoughts. He felt something was missing. He never thought he'd get so attached to her. His heart was still in the house of Mr. Ramzi, with those he cared about. Now that Farhad was on his way out, how lonely would his father feel. At least when Farhad was in Tehran he would pay their father an occasional visit; now who's going to check on the old man? He remembered when he planned to move to Isfahan his father was not happy at all. Salar would cite a thousand reasons for Kaveh to stay in Tehran and in that house. But he didn't want to stay in Ramzi's house any longer. He relied on his intellect and his physical strength. Despite his hunched back, he had always been tough. He constantly remembered his father's words… *"Three things in life create power: knowledge, wealth, and beauty."* And Kaveh needed to have the first two.

When he was admitted to the University of Agriculture, he told Salar he wanted to move to Isfahan, study there and work on his uncle's farm. Knowing Kaveh had made up his mind, Salar didn't keep insisting and agreed to his wishes despite his own misgivings.

Kaveh was sharp and capable. He knew why he'd come to Isfahan and what he wanted to accomplish there. He visited his uncle's ranch as soon as he was finished with the university, but what he saw shocked him.

The land resembled an arid desert. Nothing was planted there. The old farmhand, Moosa, told him his uncle is busy as a trader in the Isfahan bazar and has abandoned the farm.

Kaveh started working immediately. He hired a few assistants through Moosa; brought in a mechanic to fix the idle and broken tractor; built two rooms for himself, and took up residence on the ranch. It didn't take long for him to turn that barren farm into a paradise famous to everyone around. A year later, the farm started to yield crops. His uncle, who loved him dearly, put a section of the land in his name as gratitude for his efforts. Kaveh told him he would only accept if they signed a contract and he could pay for the land in installments.

It didn't take long for the farm to start harvesting. Kaveh opened a livestock business alongside the ranch. More workers were hired and the business flourished to the point where it began exporting milk and other dairy products to the nearby areas and even Isfahan. Kaveh had now become one of Isfahan's wealthy elite and was thinking about building a township, and that is why he asked Soodabeh for help in drawing the designs.

But now that he'd amassed great wealth, he felt he was searching for something more. The money, land, business and even the coming township with its huge revenue potential did not fulfill him. He was an austere and ascetic person. Despite his wealth, he still lived in the same two-room cottage. He loved the soil and the wheat fields. The sounds of the cattle and the rooster's crow in the early morning pleased him. He was after the essence of existence. He tried to search within himself, pull back the layers of his identity and discover his true desires and innate talents. He believed this to be the way for mankind to get closer to its core. In his view, the creative and ingenious are intellectuals who don't simply conform. He believed humans cannot think identically and cannot be equal in all subjects; a person devoid of intellectual creativity could never pose as a creative thinker. In the words of Ayn Rand, the

American philosopher and novelist, if we liken our bodies to an automobile and see our thoughts and ideas as the driver, those who lack thoughts and insight are like cars moving without a driver, always in danger of crashing. Just the same, someone who refuses to think and takes matters too lightly resembles an idle car that will gradually break down. Furthermore, an individual who allows others to decide for him and is simply a follower brings to mind a car being towed by another vehicle. Once a person idolizes another and becomes his devotee, he resembles those who need someone else's car to get to their destination.

Simply put, humans are alive to the extent of their ingenuity. It was for this reason that Kaveh relied exclusively on his own intellect, will and tenacity and had trust in his ultimate success. Throughout college he had been acquainted with various political beliefs such as communism, socialism and absolutism, but he hadn't bought into any of them. He considered his own views and beliefs as superior to those of groups that wanted him as a follower.

Despite being committed to reason and practicality, he also had a strong belief in human emotions and true love, and was always careful not to make a mistake in attaining this divine gift. This is why he hadn't declared love toward any women up to this point.

Across the sky above the farm, stars were shining brighter than ever. Kaveh, still deep in thought, remained in his chair and observed the infinite sky. The flicker of the stars drew him to the galaxies rotating in perfect order. Planet earth, mankind's habitat, was simply a small dot in this infinite universe. The greatness of creation had him shaking. He was akin to a feather caught in a windstorm. Feeling the warmth of love in his soul, he wanted to leave his body and join the cosmos. His thoughts frightened him, warmed him, intoxicated and pleased him.

Soodabeh's face wouldn't leave his mind. How delicate and pure it was; how lonely it was. His eyes burned from sleeplessness. He felt cold. He had been sitting there for hours. He slowly left his seat, picked up a rose brought by

Soodabeh from the garden and smelled it; how fragrant it was. He took it with him to his room. Filling a glass with water, he placed the rose inside and left it on the table next to his bed. He removed his clothes and fell on the bed, pulled the blanket over himself and slept like a baby.

....

The night before Farhad's flight to America, he heard the doorbell ring just as he was packing his last suitcase. Opening the door, he saw Kaveh standing before him. He was startled; they hadn't seen each other in two years. Besides, he had already said goodbye to him over the phone. What could have possibly brought his brother to Tehran?

"Don't be nervous my brother," said Kaveh, detecting Farhad's surprise and concern. "I'm here to say goodbye in person. Since there's no telling when you'll be back, I just wanted to see you one more time."

The brothers hugged each other. Farhad offered a seat to Kaveh.

"So you're leaving after all."

"Yes, I'm finally going." Farhad replied, smiling and sad at the same time.

"You're going to a good place for a good purpose." Kaveh said happily.

Farhad's lips tightened. "But my heart is here."

"Then why don't you take the person you love with you?"

Farhad walked toward the kitchen. "We tried hard to get her a visa, but it didn't work out. I would have loved for us to go together. I love Manijheh so much."

"Do you love her enough to not go if she asks you to stay?"

Farhad paused, thought for a second, and then said with conviction, "I love her and my heart will stay with her, but I have to go. I have to continue my research. Technology has really advanced in America. Opportunity there is plenty. I have some ideas that if developed can answer so many unsolved mysteries."

Seeing Farhad had his mind set, Kaveh stood. "Wonderful. Just one thing: wherever you are, never forget the essence and foundation of humanity."

After Kaveh bid him farewell, Farhad was left wondering if his brother had really come just to say goodbye. Had he come to dissuade him from leaving?

The next day Farhad left for America.

....

Laura's Blue Eyes

Farhad was seated across from the chairman of the physics department at Columbia University. Winter snow was visible outside the window. The chairman, an elderly man with gray hair and glasses, sat behind an ebony desk, carefully reviewing Farhad's documents. The room was pleasantly warm. Farhad was trying to present a calm exterior despite his anxiety and tension;

this meeting was extremely vital since failing to gain admission would have ruined all his plans. At that moment the chairman's response meant more to him than anything in the world.

Finally, after a while that seemed like a century, the chairman raised his head. "Your academic background is quite impressive," he said, handing back Farhad's papers. "It is compatible with the type of research we do here at Columbia." Farhad felt elated and listened excitedly. The man added, "Dr. Laura Parker has written a few articles on the same topics and is currently involved in electromagnetic research."

As he spoke, he wrote a couple of phone numbers on a piece of paper and handed it to Farhad. "You can work with her."

Farhad stood and took the paper. "So you're hiring me?" he asked eagerly.

"That will be determined by the administrative department," the chairman replied calmly. "You need to give them your credentials. If they approve, you can start working here."

Farhad looked at the note. One number belonged to Dr. Parker and the other to administration. He picked up his papers, thanked the chairman and left the room. He was beside himself with joy.

It was snowing outside, but inside Farhad spring was taking root. The professors and students walked the halls, each heading in a different direction. Farhad, with the note in hand, headed for the information booth. From there he called Laura Parker. She picked up personally. Farhad introduced himself, added he had been instructed to call by the department chairman, and asked to set up a meeting.

"Well why don't you stop by my office right now?" said Laura.

Farhad went there enthusiastically. Upon entering the room, what he saw astounded him; Laura was a young woman of striking beauty. She rose from her seat to greet Farhad and welcomed him warmly.

"I've been here for a week," said Farhad. "I came from Iran hoping to get hired at Columbia."

He showed her his credentials. Laura carefully examined them and began to read one of his articles. The room was quiet. Farhad kept his cool but couldn't help admiring this woman. After a while, Dr. Parker looked up and smiled kindly. "We both work on the same topic. If we collaborate, we could definitely get faster results." She then paused and added, "I was going to get lunch at the cafeteria. If you haven't eaten yet, join me so we can get to know each other better."

Feeling hungry, Farhad accepted and they took off. Seated together at a less crowded part of the cafeteria, Laura asked him, "Have you seen New York?"

"Not yet. I'm familiar with the neighborhood I live in, but the place I really want to see is the Statue of Liberty."

Laura looked at him sympathetically. "Most immigrants come to this country for the freedom."

"I was already free in my country. I'm here for my goals."

The more Laura conversed with him the more she came to respect his views; Farhad's poise and character impressed her. After lunch she gave him her mobile number and told him to call if he has any problems. Once they separated, Farhad left for the office of administration. He was met by an older woman who seemed to be in charge. He informed her of his reasons for being there and handed over his documents. The lady, Doris, scrutinized the papers but apparently couldn't find what she was searching for. Finally she looked up. "May I see your Green Card?"

"I have a tourist visa, not a permanent resident card."

"We can't hire you without a Green Card or a student visa." Doris shook her head apologetically.

"Well what am I supposed to do now?" Farhad asked anxiously.

"I think you need to speak to an attorney and apply for a Green Card."

She returned the documents to Farhad. When he left the room, it was sunny and the snow had stopped, but his heart was clouded with disappointment. He had no idea what to do. He didn't know anyone and didn't have much money. He only had a few months to obtain a Green Card or student visa, otherwise this opportunity was lost.

He spent that night thinking and worrying. Early the next morning he called Laura and told her the story. She set up a time for them to meet and promised to talk to an attorney she knew. In the meantime, Farhad headed into New York City. He walked the crowded streets teeming with skyscrapers. As he moved around the congested town, he was reminded of his memories of Tehran: those days of romance and restlessness, of unforgettable exhilaration and sweet memories.

But at that moment on the streets of New York, a major dilemma weighed on his mind. He had to gain admission to Columbia at any cost. He was willing to pay the price no matter how steep! He had researched all the matters involved in obtaining a Green Card. He was too smart not to know the obstacles in the way, especially for an Iranian. But he was certain he would succeed.

It was this exact willpower and tenacity that distinguished him from others. He was well aware that individuals can determine their fate through their decisions; yes, he knew this quite well. He believed that man is measured by his intellect and that his stature is directly related to his acumen. Discerning right from wrong; reason and logic; these are the exclusive domain of mankind. Otherwise animals are just as capable of instinctive behavior.

He had no doubt that in creation humans are innately endowed with intelligence, common sense, wisdom, and inevitably, free will. These gifts are all tools for attaining spiritual perfection which is the foundation and essence of existence. He knew that wisdom and spirituality are the building blocks of man, and was certain that spiritual enlightenment is only possible through canonized guidance, but was there a way to prove this through science as well? This is the question Farhad had in mind and sought the answer to. Achieving this goal through the scientific method, and finding an opening – no matter how little – into the mysteries of the hidden world was favorable, and the costs didn't seem to matter.

Captivated by these ideas, he continued his stroll through New York. Thinking of Laura's beautiful face and her kindness toward him as a newcomer warmed his heart. He kept looking up at the towering Manhattan buildings as he passed by the shops and restaurants. The streets of New York were congested and jam-packed much like those in Tehran. The crowd moved about at a rapid pace. The passing of cars and yellow cabs and the roar of the underground trains were maddening. The air wasn't too polluted but it sure was frosty. To escape the winter cold, Farhad sought refuge in a café along the way.

The place was small and most tables were taken, but he found a small one and sat down. He ordered a bowl of soup and a sandwich and started looking around. The young couples dining and chatting reminded him of himself and Manijheh in those last few days in Tehran. His heart felt heavy, but he knew he had to control his emotions. Right now, his one and only love had to be his goal and he had to overcome all obstacles in the way. A vague sadness burdened him. He sighed and stood up; it was time to meet Laura and he needed to get to her office as soon as possible. On the way there, he remembered his father's words when they last met: *"Your mother made me promise to encourage you toward a college education."* There was no way he could return to Iran empty handed; now he felt even more determined to stay. Arriving at Laura's office, he found her conversing with a young colleague.

As soon as she saw Farhad she walked over and greeted him warmly. "Come meet Dr. Albert!" She turned to the doctor. "This Iranian scientist is new here. His research is incredible and he has a bright future. He speaks English quite well too. But he has some problems with residency and university rules won't allow him to get hired. He doesn't have much time left to get his Green Card."

Dr. Albert was tall and handsome. After exchanging pleasantries with Farhad, he told him with a meaningful smile, "Your problem could be solved by marrying an American woman."

Hearing this, Laura looked at Farhad enthusiastically, hoping to see his reaction to the suggestion. But his face was completely expressionless!

Following Dr. Albert's departure, Farhad and Laura chatted for a while. As it was getting close to dinnertime, she invited him to eat together and he accepted without reservation. At the restaurant there was no more talk of work, employment or visa issues. Their discussions shifted toward getting to know each other, their backgrounds, and comparing their cultures and personal interests. Farhad told Laura about his reasons for immigration and his dreams of staying in America to pursue his research at Columbia. Listening to him attentively, she promised to do all she can to help him gain admission to the university.

When saying goodbye, she squeezed his hand. "You must stay here."

"I definitely will," replied Farhad, unable to avert his eyes from her.

....

On his way back to the hotel, Farhad received a call from Manijheh. Her voice sounded down and dejected. He became worried. "What's the matter, Manijheh?"

"Nothing. I just really miss you."

Farhad still sounded concerned. "You'll drive me insane one day."

"What about you?" she replied with a bit of coquetry. "You drove me insane from day one."

He asked about the family and Soodabeh and then informed her that things were starting to work out.

"So you're staying then." She sounded disappointed.

"You're starting this again?" replied Farhad, a bit agitated. "Didn't we already go over all this?" Then to stop her from pursuing the argument, he added, "I'll be renting an apartment soon; the hotel cost is too high. You'll be able to call the house then. If I can't answer the phone sometimes it's because I'm either in a meeting or my phone is off."

"I wish I was in that house with you," Manijheh said wistfully.

Farad said nothing, but seeing the cab stop at the hotel, he told her goodbye.

From the time Farhad had arrived in America, Manijheh had called and emailed on a daily basis and even sent two letters each week. Despite being busy, Farhad tried to answer her calls and respond to her emails as often as possible but she still wasn't content.

....

Four months had now passed since Farhad's arrival in New York. His residency permit was still on hold, but he'd been able to rent an apartment near Columbia with Laura's assistance. She had also helped him decorate the place and furnish it. Every once in a while they would meet there and spend some time together.

From the day they met, Farhad had been impressed by Laura's beauty. In the few months they had spent socializing he had found her to be intelligent and thoughtful as well, and her tireless efforts to assist him made Farhad feel even closer to her. She would challenge him in all discussions; something Manijheh had never done due to her tendency to always go along with his opinions. He was now dealing with a woman who stimulated his mind and motivated him to think better and analyze more. These appealing traits made Laura even more desirable to Farhad. He could sense himself getting closer and closer to her and farther and farther away from Manijheh.

Manijheh, on the other hand, persisted with her emails and phone calls. Farhad tried to not respond to her calls when Laura was around. He had shared many things about his past with the American woman, but had never mentioned Manijheh. He was now stuck at a crossroads.

One late afternoon in autumn, Laura contacted Farhad and set up a meeting at their usual hangout in Manhattan, saying she wanted to discuss his residency.

She had been interested in him from the day he set foot in her office; their subsequent meetings had only made her more attracted to him. As she became more familiar with Farhad and his eastern charisma, she fell head over heels. Even more importantly, his knowledge and extraordinary dedication to scientific research compelled her to keep Farhad in America at all costs and perhaps even start a life with him. She had spoken to a few attorneys, she had done all she could to obtain a scholarship for him at Columbia, but nothing was working. The days were going by quickly and Farhad's visa was about to expire. Laura had to come up with a plan.

That night she looked stunning. Her tight black dress, wavy hair draped over her shoulders, blue eyes and inviting smile all set Farhad's heart aflutter. He could not take his eyes off of her. He was so captivated that he couldn't remember why she had asked to see him in the first place.

Seated across from Laura, still mesmerized by her allure, he heard her voice fill his ears like the echoes of a divine instrument. "Are you alright?"

He knew he wasn't, but said nothing and continued to stare. Having detected Farhad's condition, she continued, "Tonight marks the fifth month of your stay in the country. There isn't much time left on your visa. I've had talks with several attorneys so far to get you some type of residency or scholarship but nothing has come of them. I don't really know what to do. I truly want to see you hired at Columbia but I have no idea how it can be done."

Farhad looked grim. Laura's words felt like blows of a hammer. "What am I to do?" he asked dejectedly. "Leave everything and go back? What about my research?"

Laura seemed to have been waiting for that exact question. "I've spoken to one of Dr. Albert's friends who is an immigration lawyer. He says the quickest way to receive a Green Card is through marrying an American citizen."

Farhad was speechless, feeling as if the ground had been pulled from under him. "You can always go back to your country," said Laura resentfully, observing his expression.

"No, I don't want to go back," he answered in a panic. "I came here with great goals in mind..."

"To reach great goals you have to sacrifice some things," Laura said with a hint of indifference. At that moment their food arrived. "Let's just eat for now."

Farhad had no appetite; he only poured himself some soda and drank. He had a lump in his throat. Manijheh's face kept running across his mind. He couldn't forget that angelic face and her words the last time he saw her: *"You'll go and forget about me."*

Laura looked him over for a moment. She touched his hand gently. "Don't think about it too much. It'll work out eventually."

Farhad glanced at her pale, petite hands, then raised his head and looked into her deep blue eyes. Her loving gaze was exhilarating, the warmth of her hands reassuring. As if something had just occurred to him, he said, "What am I to do then?"

She let go of his hand. "We Americans don't beat around the bush like you Easterners. When we want something done, we do it. I'm willing to marry you, because I actually love you as well."

Farhad remained quiet but showed his agreement by nodding his head.

Laura went on. "We have one month left; let's get to know each other better. My parents live in Washington. We'll go for a visit so you can meet them and they can find out about you as well." She paused for a second and then added, "Talk a little bit about yourself."

Farhad didn't know where to start. Should he begin with his father who was a butler for the Ramzis? Or with the Ramzi family? Perhaps Manijheh? He left all that alone. "My objective is what's important to me," he said. "There is no doubt in my mind that carrying on my studies will help me find the keys to some major mysteries. The advanced technology here can help me overcome some of the complications in my research. I can't let a visa stand in the way of my goals."

"Then let's get married so your residency is taken care of," implored Laura, impressed by Farhad's resolve.

Farhad spent that night at her place.

Their wedding was hosted in Washington by Laura's parents. The guest list consisted entirely of her friends, family and colleagues. No one from the groom's side was present. None of them even knew!

Upon returning from their honeymoon in Hawaii, Laura contacted the lawyer she knew and handed him their marriage certificate. A short while later Farhad officially joined the Columbia research team.

After marrying Laura, Farhad no longer found a reason to contact Iran. He seemed to avoid his memories. The only reminders of Manijheh were her photos and that book of Hafez she'd given him as a keepsake before he left. With sadness and grief, Farhad placed those in a box and hid them among the personal items in his closet. It was as if he intended to bury all his memories in there.

Before changing his phone number, he contacted his father and without mentioning Laura, simply gave him the news of his entry to Columbia and his great position there. He also stated he'd be quite busy for a while working and traveling around America, so he wouldn't be able to keep in constant communication with Iran. For the first time ever, he had lied to Salar! For all intents and purposes he had burned all bridges behind him. He was prepared to start a new life across the oceans and pursue his dreams. Because as Laura said, to achieve great objectives one must forego certain things.

....

Where Were You When I Lay in Ruins

It had been exactly four weeks since Manijheh last heard of Farhad. After he'd left for America they had spoken on the phone every day. She emailed him daily and wrote two letters each week as well, but now they hadn't had any contact in a month. She asked about him a few times from Salar, but he told her he didn't know either and guessed that Farhad could be traveling for scientific seminars. But Manijheh didn't believe any of it and had an ominous feeling.

She wasn't feeling well physically either. She was weak and out of sorts, dealing with frequent dizziness, nausea and rapid weight gain. She could tell she was pregnant. A clinical examination confirmed it. She didn't know whether this made her happy or concerned. On the one hand she was nurturing within her the product of her love with Farhad, but on the other hand, he might never return and marry her; then what would become of her?

Throughout the month she had spent agonizing over Farhad and deteriorating physically, Soodabeh had spoken to her frequently and was clearly concerned, but Manijheh told her nothing. Finding it impossible to watch her sister in that condition and do nothing, Soodabeh reached out to Auntie who promised to find out exactly what was happening. On one occasion the aunt got a hold of Manijheh and chatted with her extensively, but no information was forthcoming, not even about losing contact with Farhad. Soodabeh and her aunt decided to keep an eye on things and Manijheh continued to remain secretive.

Five months had now passed since Farhad left Iran. Now Manijheh had to make a decision, as her pregnancy was no longer concealable. One late afternoon she went to the park near their house. Anxious and apprehensive, she sat there and reflected for quite some time. She had to get in touch with Farhad somehow; even if it meant going to America. It was dark now and a light rain was pouring down. She thought, "I'll call him one last time" and hopelessly dialed the number she had left repeated messages on before. She hadn't called his cell phone since Farhad told her to stop. This time the call didn't go to voice mail. A woman speaking English was on the other end. Since she spoke English well herself, Manijheh asked with suspicion, "Can I speak to Farhad?"

"Yes."

"Who are you?"

"I'm his wife," Laura answered.

Manijheh felt weak from head to toe. Her heart was racing but she did her best to keep calm. She told herself she must have misheard. "May I speak to Farhad?" she asked one more time in a faint voice.

"Of course." Laura called out to Farhad, "The call is for you."

Moments later, Manijheh heard his voice. "Yes, this is Farhad. You are?"

"Is this lady telling the truth about being your wife?" asked Manijheh abruptly.

Recognizing her voice, his heart sank. He said nothing. "Answer me!" She screamed.

"I had no choice but to marry her." Farhad sounded apologetic. "There was no other way to get a Green Card. They wouldn't let me work at the university..."

Manijheh felt disoriented. She couldn't hear him anymore. The phone fell out of her hand and she left the park not knowing what she was doing. She had lost control of her thoughts and actions; something had died inside her. Her limbs trembled. She could feel the fetus kicking inside. Every fiber of her being was on fire. It was now raining harder and she was soaking wet. In an instance, all her hopes and dreams had been lost. She had believed her love with Farhad was eternal and indestructible; now it crushed her to realize she had given her heart to someone unfit and unworthy. How silly and stupid she had been to not figure this until now. Her sobs were muffled by the sound of the rain washing away her tears. Nothing mattered anymore. Her love was shattered; the person she adored had betrayed her... She felt worthless knowing she had given her all to someone who had disposed of her so casually; she hated herself. Not knowing how or why, she was now in the middle of the street. Suddenly she heard the loud thud of metal hitting her and all went black.

When she opened her eyes, she found herself on a hospital bed. A lady dressed in white was telling her softly, "It's time to wake up now. The operation went well. You'll get better soon."

"My child?" asked Manijheh. Her voice was faint, barely audible.

The nurse's expression saddened. "It couldn't be saved," she said gently.

Manijheh turned her head away as two teardrops rolled down her face. The nurse tried to console her but Manijheh could hear nothing. When they took her to her room Salar was there waiting. Seeing her, he put his head down. He had heard about the accident back at the house and got there as fast as he could. Manijheh was in the operating room when he arrived. He just sat there and prayed. When he heard the baby was lost, it was as if the world had crashed down on him; he had no doubt it belonged to Farhad. His head in his hands, he had no idea what to do. As soon as he heard Manijheh was taken back to her room he rushed over.

After Goli's passing, all other hardships had been easy to handle. He hadn't been seriously tested since. But tonight he felt desperate and despondent. The only thing on his mind was being there for Manijheh and helping her get through this ordeal. He had raised her himself and knew her mentality well. Unlike Soodabeh, she was delicate and fragile and the slightest adversity crushed her. Salar had to help somehow, but in what way? It wasn't easy to tell a woman who had been abandoned by the father of her child that her baby was now lost too. His legs felt weak and his heart raced.

When Manijheh turned her head away in the room, the weight of the world came down on him; he knew his grandchild was gone... He sat beside Manijheh. "Why didn't you tell me!? You know I love you more than life itself. Why didn't you share your secret?"

Manijheh still faced the other way.

"Now at least let me share your pain. I beg you... Don't deny this of me."

She still wouldn't look at him. Salar squeezed her blanket. His voice trembled. "Just let me see your kind eyes one more time."

At that point Manijheh turned to him, staring blankly. Salar kissed her eyes and hands. "Thank you". He then phoned Soodabeh from the hospital.

Within a half hour, Soodabeh and Auntie arrived in a panic. Ahmad Ramzi and his son Farshid were in Dubai on business and were not yet informed. Both women were speechless upon hearing the news. Soodabeh sat by Manijheh's bed and embraced her as she sobbed. "The world doesn't stay this way," she consoled her sister while caressing her hair. "Anyone who breaks a heart will have their own torn to a thousand pieces."

Auntie stood next to Salar and remained silent, knowing what he was going through. She had faith in his purity and integrity but didn't know what could be done. She couldn't see how Manijheh was going to come to terms with this calamity, and worse yet, how it could be kept from Ramzi who had just started to recover from financial troubles and would have been wiped out without Kaveh's assistance.

Soon after Farhad's exit, Ahmad Ramzi had fallen on hard times in his business to an extent that had alarmed the family. They could see him return from the factory depressed and dejected, always heading straight to his room to study the papers he'd brought back with him. He had been distancing himself from the rest of the house. Auntie was the first to notice something was wrong. The truth was that his factory was on the verge of bankruptcy and his assets were nearly wiped out. He had even been forced to leverage his house and borrow large sums of money. With his factory still in bad shape, his lenders had begun to exert pressure. Given that his outlook on life was based purely on wealth and affluence, Ramzi fell into a deep depression. He could not see a way out of his predicament. After a period of rumination he decided to call on an old friend in the trade ministry. He had previously hosted this top official and held many feasts in his honor. The official greeted him warmly and asked about his reason for coming. Ramzi described some of his troubles and asked for assistance in obtaining a generous loan. Upon hearing this request, the official's demeanor changed; his smile disappeared and his expression turned cold. "Give me a little time to investigate this further and return next week for an answer." It was clear he was trying to end the meeting.

He then said goodbye to Ramzi and almost pushed him out the door. Despite the blatant disrespect, Ramzi remained hopeful for a positive outcome in the next meeting. He spent the entire week in the house and tried to hide from the lenders. On the day of the appointment, he wore a brand new suit and headed to his friend's office. The secretary, who already knew him, claimed the official was in a meeting and unable to see anyone. "Unfortunately they were unable to accommodate your request," was the message she relayed.

No matter how much he tried, Ramzi could not see the official that day. He finally returned home, angry and resentful at being belittled in this manner.

Auntie was there when he arrived. From his expression she could tell he was upset. He sat in the living room and she brought him a glass of water. He then asked her to call Salar over.

Salar entered minutes later. Ramzi offered him a seat. "Salar, I want to share something with you," said Ramzi without any pretense. "I'm bankrupt, my factory is almost lost. I'm in debt to many people and may end up in jail soon. Before any of that happens, I want to settle my account with you. Believe me; losing you saddens me greatly. But there is nothing I can do. My hands are tied."

Salar smiled. "You think the salary is the reason I've stayed here all these years? This is my home; I don't feel like a stranger here. I don't want your money."

"This house is leveraged to the factory. I will lose this too. Everything's lost. I have too much debt to too many people."

"Well, we can go to my house," Salar replied. "We'll live there."

"Your house?" Ramzi looked surprised.

"Yes, the house Kaveh bought me is a few blocks from here. It's large and roomy."

Ramzi looked at him in shock. His sister who had been listening to their conversation had tears in her eyes.

"You're too worried about material things," said Salar. "How much of it do you think you'll take with you? It's been a while since you came to my room and we had tea together. Let's go there now, let me read you a story from Shahnameh."

Then without waiting for Ramzi to respond, he left the room.

A week after this conversation, Kaveh showed up at Ramzi's factory. "Tell Mr. Ramzi that Kaveh, Salar's son, is here to see him," he told the secretary.

At the factory Salar was well known and well respected. The secretary welcomed Kaveh cordially and headed straight for Ramzi's office. Within a few minutes Ramzi came out. Seeing Kaveh surprised him! But he greeted him affectionately and led him to his office.

Kaveh was limping more than usual. Ahmad Ramzi sat behind his desk and offered him a chair across from it. His legs hurting, he sat down with difficulty. After a few seconds he locked eyes with Ramzi. "Mr. Ramzi, perhaps you're surprised by me being here," said Kaveh in a friendly tone. "To be honest, when I heard about your factory's situation, I thought it's time for me to come through for you. I have a proposal."

Ahmad Ramzi stared at him attentively. "What kind of proposal?"

"I hear your factory is not doing well. I know how mismanagement and negligence have ruined Iranian commerce. How are you supposed to sell your aluminum dishes at even the manufacturing price when similar Chinese products are available for half that amount? This is all due to a lack of proper economic policies. The majority of officials are also irresponsible and indifferent, so help can't be expected from them."

Kaveh paused for a moment. "But I have a lot of ideas for your factory," he added. "I'd like to buy half the ownership and pay all your debt as a loan. The truth of the matter is, other than the farm and livestock and other businesses, I also have some capital sitting in the bank. You also have no choice but to sell your factory. I'm willing to buy, and I'll do so at a decent price."

Ramzi listened to him in amazement. Kaveh's proposal was incredible! He felt heaven's doors had opened before him. He hadn't seen Kaveh since the young man had left for the farm, but what he heard now impressed him immensely. He had known for a while that Kaveh is doing well financially, but now he could see that it wasn't due to luck, but rather economic aptitude. Kaveh observed him closely and awaited an answer.

"You're right, my dear Kaveh," said Ramzi, his peace of mind clearly returning. "I do need to sell this factory and who better than you to sell it to? I'll even retain half the ownership which I had almost given up on."

Kaveh smiled, shook Ramzi's hand and rose from his seat.

"I just want to know why you're interested in this bankrupt factory," Ramzi inquired.

"I have some plans in mind. We'll make products that can compete with the Chinese prices. It's also time to get Farshid involved; all that partying is enough."

Kaveh ended with a smile. Ramzi stood and approached him, patting him on the shoulder. "Farhad is smart and talented. But now I can see when it comes to character and compassion he has nothing on you."

"It's not about compassion," answered Kaveh with utmost humility before saying goodbye. "You're a seller and I'm a buyer."

With his substantial investment, it took less than a month for Kaveh to rescue the factory from insolvency. He met with Farshid and appointed him to oversee most of the operations. Through his business connections, he also managed to have an associate from Dubai help Ramzi and Farshid import much of what they needed.

Auntie knew telling Ramzi about Manijheh's predicament would only create further turmoil; he wasn't the type to take such matters likely. He would never forgive Farhad and might even cut ties with Salar.

Preoccupied with these thoughts, she was restless and on edge. After some deliberation, she chose to keep the matter secret and to also ask Salar and Soodabeh to do the same until Manijheh herself could decide.

Soodabeh and Manijheh were starting to calm down. Salar, standing next to Auntie, continued to watch over them. Soodabeh raised her head. Upon seeing Salar she turned to her aunt without acknowledging him. "See what happened, Auntie?"

The old lady only continued to cry quietly. "I don't want to see anyone," said Soodabeh derisively, almost yelling. "I just want to be alone with Manijheh. I want to be next to her and take care of her as long as it takes."

Shocked by the news of her sister's pregnancy and subsequent miscarriage, Soodabeh felt an incredible hatred for Farhad. Her secret feelings for him now lay shattered and the shards sliced through her soul. Farhad and everything associated with him filled her with disgust. Even Salar and Kaveh weren't exempt from her contempt.

Auntie, sensing it would be wise to leave the sisters alone, gestured at Salar to leave together. "God be with you," she told Manijheh. "I'm leaving. Call the house if you need anything."

Manijheh weakly nodded her head. But Soodabeh refused to look in Salar's direction as he left the room.

The rest of the night, she sat by her sister's side and reflected. She found it impossible to justify Farhad's actions. There could be no doubt that in his haste to chase his ambitions he had been led astray by temptation. She reached the disheartening conclusion that his rationalizations were only to appease his conscience; that school, Green Card and marriage were all but excuses. Even if the visa could not be obtained any other way, was it worth the sacrifice of one's ethics and principles?

Tormented by her sentiments, Soodabeh spent some time afterward distancing herself from Salar and even refusing to think of Kaveh. She passed the time with Manijheh, supporting and consoling her until she began to recuperate and returned home from the hospital. Ahmad Ramzi and Farshid were still in Dubai, not yet aware of the bitter events back home.

Anticipating their return, Manijheh headed to Kashan to stay with her maternal aunt in the hopes of making an emotional recovery in time to face them.

With You I'm at Peace the Most

After Manijheh left for Kashan, Salar felt out of sorts. The expansive garden and its towering trees had become a prison for him; its residents seemed like strangers. Manijheh had spent the days before her trip ignoring him, even telling him in a brief encounter, "I don't want to see you anymore, Salar. I don't want to look at anyone that reminds me of Farhad. The boy you raised I mistook for a loving man and a life companion. I threw my youth, hopes and dreams at his feet not knowing he's an evil fraud concerned only with his own interests and desires. I ask you not to face me again."

Soodabeh shunned Salar as well, avoiding his approaches every time she went home.

The sisters' treatment broke his heart. He had raised and nurtured them with heart and soul. He adored them; there was no joy in his life without them. He'd spent countless nights singing them lullabies as children, reciting tales of folk heroes till they fell asleep. But now they wouldn't even face him, although Salar could understand why. What Farhad done to the Ramzi family was unforgivable. And Salar was the one who had to pay the price for it.

One day, exhausted of pacing aimlessly around the garden, he sat under that old spruce tree where Farhad and Manijheh had carved two hearts with their names under them. Staring at the hearts, he muttered to himself, "Oh Farhad, why did you have to throw all that love and affection away? I don't know what I'd do to you if you were here!"

Auntie saw him among the trees and approached. His crushed demeanor and the long lines now visible on his forehead made her feel sorry for him. Sitting next to Salar, she tried to offer consolation. "Come on. You've been through so much in life. Why do you blame yourself? Why cry over spilt milk? Let's use common sense and find a remedy."

Salar was disconsolate. "You know how much I love Ramzi's children; they don't even want to see me now. Manijheh left for Kashan and Soodabeh keeps avoiding me. I think I need to leave this house; not because they're telling me to leave, no… because I just can't bear to look them in the eye anymore."

"Maybe Manijheh can't look you in the eyes either," said Auntie, known for her pragmatism. "She wasn't a child; she bears some responsibility too. It's not like the world has ended. Remember the gift of disremembering! Time heals all; even my broken heart… "

She sighed deeply, thinking of a wrenching memory. "When my addict husband brought his temporary wife and their child to our house, my heart broke in a thousand pieces and never mended."

Wiping a tear with her fingertip, she returned to Salar and Manijheh's dilemma. "Everyone is responsible for their own lives. What's the point in you taking the blame? Look what you've done to yourself; you've aged twenty years. Now let's go inside, Ramzi has some chores for us to do."

After that day, Salar would stay up most nights, reading the Koran and at times crying out loud. His depression had reached a point that alarmed Ramzi upon returning. "Why is Salar crying so much?" he asked Auntie.

"He's mourning his wife."

"But she's been dead for years!" And he stopped pursuing the matter.

Ever since Kaveh had saved him from bankruptcy, Ramzi was careful not to do or say anything to upset him. This is why he tolerated Salar's moodiness and odd behavior. Materialistic and greedy by nature, he liked Kaveh for financial reasons and not for who he was. Unable to overcome his avarice, he was not a good judge of character; wealth was his only criterion for respecting others. Even worse, he projected his own outlook onto everyone and believed they could be mollified the same way. Money was his God; his heart; his soul. He worshipped money and viewed all others as fellow worshippers. This delusion may have been brought on by those who flattered him for his wealth, but how ironic that those were the first to discard him like trash the moment he fell into bankruptcy.

It was this same superficial worldview that wrecked the lives of his children. Perhaps if he hadn't been so strict about Farhad and Manijheh, Farhad wouldn't have found a reason to leave in order to "return rich and marry Manijheh."

Noticing his brother had not pursued Salar's issue, Auntie cleverly changed the subject. "So, how are things going in the factory? Did Kaveh's investment make a difference?"

Ramzi, arranging his clothes in the closet, smiled broadly and turned to her. "I don't know what good I did for whom to deserve God sending me Kaveh as an angel of mercy. The factory has transformed. His intellect and drive is astounding."

Auntie saw an opportunity. "Well, it's expected of Salar to raise such a son."

Ramzi sat down. "By the way, any news from Farhad?" he asked in a serious manner. "Kaveh doesn't say much about him."

Taken aback, she quickly composed herself. "Apparently he's continuing his studies. Salar used to talk about him occasionally but hasn't said anything in a while."

Ramzi started rummaging through his briefcase, briefly interrupting their talks. "I haven't seen Soodabeh for a few days," he then said abruptly. "When I return from work she's not home, and when I'm home she's not here. Kaveh was asking about her."

"What did he want?" asked Auntie nervously. She was aware of Kaveh's feelings for Soodabeh.

"Just asked me to tell Soodabeh he needs to see her about something."

"OK. She's been busy too. Work has her very occupied."

Following Manijheh's trip to Kashan, Soodabeh was very distant with Salar. Her hatred of Farhad ran so deep that she even held his father and brother responsible for this mess; she felt they were accountable for his misdeeds.

Auntie could not ease this resentment no matter how hard she tried. Soodabeh believed Farhad had to pay for his sins one way or another. Her aunt relayed Kaveh's message to her.

One afternoon, Soodabeh came home early and waited until her father arrived. After some small talk, Ramzi complained about her not coming to see him more. She kissed him and apologized. "Believe me, I'm so consumed with problems that as soon as I come home I fall in bed and pass out."

"Sweetheart, you have been so inaccessible even Kaveh is complaining."

"Why Kaveh of all people?" she asked, surprised. "Oh, how forgetful of me," she then said in a raised voice. "I was supposed to visit his farm last week for some work on the township being built."

That night the father and daughter chatted for a couple of hours. When Soodabeh retreated to her room, she spent most of the night ruminating. On the one hand, her contempt for Farhad had led her to sever ties with Salar and Kaveh, but on the other hand, her work on Kaveh's new township required her to go to his farm.

The next night when it came time to leave for the farm, she decided to forget the anger and resentment she had developed against Salar and Kaveh. Deep down, she felt she needed to see him; what better place to reflect and be at peace than at that farm with its enchanting, starry nights?

Before leaving she paid Salar a visit. She had been apprehensive about his response, but he was beside himself with joy at seeing her. Embarrassed and not knowing what to say, she could only ask him, "I'm going to see Kaveh. Do you have any messages?"

"No, my daughter, thanks. Tell him I said hello."
He then murmured to himself. "What is there to
say…"

Soodabeh pretended not to hear.

…… …… …… …

Kaveh had just returned from horseback riding
when Moosa gave him the message. "Soodabeh
called. She's on her way here."

"When did she leave?"

"In the morning."

"She should get here soon then," said Kaveh as
he went inside in a hurry. He washed up and
changed his clothes, drank a glass of water and
waited for Soodabeh on the balcony. He sat
there for some time until the sun went down
and he started to get worried. He went into the
farm and paced around for a while, took a look
in the buildings and headed back to the house.
His legs were bothering him. A while later
Moosa saw him standing by the flowers in front
of the house, looking restless. Kaveh was
normally calm and self-controlled, unfazed by

trivial issues. But Soodabeh to him was a different matter.

Moosa approached. "Is something going on, sir? Why are you anxious?"

Kaveh didn't respond. Moosa asked again. "Sir, if there is something to be done, let me know."

"Soodabeh is late... I'm worried. Something may have happened on the way; she didn't return my calls."

"Would you like me to take the car to the edge of the road?"

"No, I'll wait another hour. If she doesn't show, I'll go myself."

It didn't take too long before Soodabeh drove to the front of the building. Kaveh went to greet her, but seeing her demeanor made his heart race. Her pale face, red eyes and dejected stare indicated something awful had happened. "What's the matter?" asked Kaveh. "Something happen on the way?" He sounded curious and concerned.

"No, the road was fine."

"Then what's the problem? Are you ill?"

"No!"

"What then?"

"Let's go in for now," said Soodabeh, distraught.

They went inside together. She sat down and he leaned against the wall. He poured her some tea. A heavy silence fell over the room. "I know I had to be here a week ago for the township business," spoke up Soodabeh. "But I wasn't feeling well. If you hadn't given the message to my father I might not have even remembered. Now that I'm here I want to stay a few days; I feel like being alone. Do you want a guest?"

Kaveh was stunned yet happy. "One of the buildings you designed is empty. I'll tell Moosa to set it up for you."

This was the building Kaveh hadn't sold and was planning to use as his office. It was close to the farm and had a great view. "So now just tell me what's going on," he asked again. "And don't beat around the bush!"

"Manijheh was in a car accident and lost her baby," said Soodabeh bluntly.

Kaveh grimaced. "She was pregnant?"

"Five months!"

"By Farhad?"

"Yes."

"Has she told him?"

"She called, and his wife picked up the phone."

Kaveh went silent, but his eyes seethed with rage and contempt.

"I want to be away from everyone for a few days," said Soodabeh. "To be honest I didn't even want to come here; seeing anyone that reminds me of Farhad torments me!"

"You have every right. If I was in your shoes I'd be sickened by Farhad and his family too. But try and stay here." He went on. "I'm sorry! Farhad wasn't the person you thought he was. That has to be hard to accept."

He then picked up Soodabeh's bag and they headed toward the buildings.

Kaveh had a unique character that couldn't be judged by ordinary standards. His nature pure and his spirit enlightened, he was faithful in love and committed to his word. He never broke his vows and didn't treat human qualities as commodities. He knew love is an exquisite jewel that outshines impurity and elevates the soul.

He accompanied Soodabeh to the building and then called over Moosa. "Bring her food and see to it that she gets whatever she needs," he requested, instructing him to take care of her living arrangements for the next few days.

He then went back to the house, sat on the balcony and phoned Salar. "Soodabeh is here. She told me everything. How are you keeping up?"

Salar's voice was barely audible. "I'm living moment to moment. We'll see how it turns out." He then added, "Keep any eye on Soodabeh; she's been in agony this whole time.

I'm not feeling well right now. I'll call you later."

After hanging up, Kaveh spent a few hours on the balcony, deep in thought.

The next three days, Soodabeh remained inside and Kaveh was anxious and on edge. The pain in his legs and the hump on his back were now compounded by the distress over Soodabeh. She had become reclusive and unwilling to eat, as if she'd given up on the world altogether. He went over to her several times and did his best to offer hope and support.

He was sleepless most nights as well. Moosa spotted him a few times sitting outside on the stairs by himself thinking. He had never seen Kaveh this upset before. One late night, observing him outside again, he told Abdol standing guard at the farm, "Mr. Kaveh has lost his mind over this girl?!!"

On the third day, Soodabeh received a call to go to Shiraz. She went to the window facing the farm. Opening it, the cool breeze against her face filled her with joy; it was as if she'd been jolted from her stupor. She caught a glimpse of Farhad walking outside and felt butterflies dance in her stomach. He noticed her too. She waved and smiled. Seeing him overwhelmed her with delight; something told her the only motivation she had left to stay in the world was Kaveh's presence.

Minutes later, bag in hand, she stood before him as he leaned against the tree outside the house. Kaveh could see how gaunt and emaciated she'd become. "You're finally outside!"

"I have to go to Shiraz for a seminar," answered Soodabeh calmly.

"When are you coming back?"

"I don't know. I might not come back here."

Kaveh looked disappointed. "Alright, go, but come back. Just return any time you want."

As they walked toward her car, Soodabeh told him she'll send the work papers from Tehran.

He watched with sadness as she drove away. Soodabeh was a fountain of love and affection and he hated to see her go.

....

One of Kaveh's friends in the area was Mr. Saeed Erfan, a high school literature instructor whom he called on occasionally when uncertain about an issue. In his free time Mr. Erfan would often pay Kaveh a visit and they would chat at the farmhouse, or spend some afternoons having tea on the balcony and discussing the day's events. That day Kaveh went to see him again. If there was one person who could help him make sense of things now it was Mr. Erfan, especially given his own sentimental nature. Kaveh had more or less told him his life story, and Mr. Erfan, familiar with his admirable character, held Kaveh in high regard. Upon seeing him, Mr. Erfan could tell something was wrong. He welcomed him with open arms and they headed into the living room. With the Erfan family away on vacation, Kaveh felt free to open up and disclose the secret weighing on his heart. A few minutes passed in silence while

Mr. Erfan prepared some tea. Despite having some clues about the issue he remained silent as they had their tea and sweets, allowing Kaveh to speak when he was ready.

Kaveh finally broke the silence, reciting the poem:

> *It's me and the burnt candle of my heart,*
> *assist me lord...*

Mr. Erfan could now read his mind and answered in kind:

> *I've spent the night begging fortune to*
> *grant the dawn   So that I*
> *may begin telling you the tale of my woes*

Kaveh laughed wholeheartedly. "Indeed, you said exactly what I intended."

"Yes, romance has a legend of its own," said Mr. Erfan, a worldly man. "One that is astounding, mysterious and stirring. A person not acquainted with love is not likely to know mercy. As Hafez says:

> *Drowned in the sea of sin from a hundred*
> *sides, though I be*

Since I became love's friend, of the people of mercy am I"

"Yes, dear Saeed," said Kaveh upon hearing this. "I am indeed one of the people of mercy."

"Who has lit this fire inside you?" enquired Mr. Erfan.

"I didn't even know till today how much love has overtaken me," answered Kaveh with a lump in his throat.

"Well, what's the problem then? Who can actually know you and not give you their heart?"

"I sense she has strong feelings for someone else."

Mr. Erfan patted him on the shoulder. "Listen my friend; this world with all its order and beauty is but a symbol of the kindness, benevolence, knowledge, power and wisdom of the creator," he said gently. "What is now in your path is undoubtedly by divine goodwill; simply carry on with your usual poise and composure. The chess pieces are set; just pick the best one to make a play with. As Aristotle believes: every good deed brings about our bliss; every worthy effort is a precursor to the wisdom that our happiness depends upon. To arrive at happiness, we must attain that wisdom."

Kaveh understood well what his scholarly friend spoke about. He learned that night that he must conquer his inner turmoil through patience.

....

This is no longer my house

Manijheh spent a month at her aunt's home in Kashan. Her depression and misery had alarmed her aunt. She spent the majority of the time secluded and immersed in her thoughts, sitting for long periods in a corner and staring at the walls. Her aunt perceived this to be a result of the accident and did her best to nurse her back to health.

Manijheh was still unable to forget those carefree days of bliss spent at Farhad's side. How could he so quickly have forgotten their oaths and promises? No. This wasn't acceptable and did not make sense by any standard of morals and principles. Losing her child, the fruit of her pure and untainted love for Farhad, burned her to the core. She felt as though her heart had been torn apart and she had no clue how to mend the pieces together again. In crowds, she was quiet and miserable; in solitude, she wept bitterly.

Her friend, Farry, called her once a day to ease the pain of loneliness. Farry insisted for Manijheh to return to Tehran as soon as possible, but she just wasn't ready emotionally. While doing her best to comfort her friend, Farry was angry that Manijheh had given herself so naively to Farhad.

A month of seclusion in Kashan and mourning in solitude restored some calm to Manijheh. Enduring all the pain and misfortune had now made her more resigned and at peace. Little by little, she was forgetting about Farhad and burying her love for him deep in her heart. She felt lighter now; what other choices did she have but surrender and acceptance?

A chapter in her life was now closed and it was time to write new ones. She left for Tehran with no intention of sharing with her father the tragedy she'd endured, since the only possible outcome would be his pain and mental anguish.

When she entered the orchard, Salar was the first person she saw. He was watering the flowers. She simply said hello. He ran toward her and showered her with kind words. "I wish I'd known you were coming; I would have sacrificed a lamb for you."

She gave him an ice cold stare. "Your son sacrificed me, my child, and my life. That's more than enough."

He simply looked at her. She noticed him breaking, crumbling, but said nothing. She'd never seen him this way before. Without saying another word, she walked to the house.

No one was inside other than Auntie. Upon seeing Manijheh, she screamed and they embraced each other affectionately.

....

The day after Manijheh returned to Tehran, her friend Farry came to visit. Farry was ecstatic to see her friend back and to see her life returning to normal, although deep down she felt Manijheh bore some responsibility for her dilemma as well. In any case, during their talks, Farry mentioned that she'd met the man she'd been looking for and they were planning a big engagement party which she invited Manijheh to. Despite her reluctance to take part in any festivities, Manijheh's friendship with Farry was too important for her to miss the ceremony.

Since falling on turbulent times, Manijheh had all but given up on personal grooming and make-up. However on Farry's engagement day she decided to keep up appearances, prepare for the party and dress appropriately. She wore an elegant black gown with white ribbons and mesh adorning its collar and cuffs. Her chic stilettos complemented her figure nicely and her blonde hair was pulled back. Still, her face looked a bit sad.

Entering the hall, she observed a large group of college classmates and family friends socializing around the room. Some light music played in the background. The banquet hall was spacious with tall windows opening to the balcony. A large multi-level cake, stylishly decorated, sat on one table while roses and orchids arranged on the others filled the room with their signature scent. Upon arriving she noticed Dariush standing in a crowd and listening to their conversation with interest. He was tall, well dressed and his dark hair hung charmingly over his forehead. His gaze was relaxed and calm, his movements measured and dignified. When he saw Manijheh his eyes lit up. He said hi from the distance but then rejoined the group he was chatting with. Given his previous enthusiasm when meeting her, Manijheh was startled by his apparent indifference now. Nevertheless, her good looks had already attracted plenty of attention. She knew Farry liked Dariush's personality and had invited him mainly for them to get to know each other better.

After dinner and before cutting the engagement cake, Dariush approached Manijheh and sat next to her. "Well, I guess now we have to get to know each other a little more," he said in a calm tone.

His voice sounded very confident. This made Manijheh more relaxed, and they chatted for a while. Farry was very happy to see them together; she knew Dariush could be a great support for her friend.

From that day on, Manijheh and Dariush would see each other at parties and events, and occasionally met for lunch or dinner at a restaurant. She enjoyed his company very much, and Soodabeh and Auntie were pleased to see her happy and active again. Dariush, who had fancied Manijheh since day one and took every opportunity to be near her, gradually became her good friend and companion.

Manijheh saw her sister Soodabeh less often now due to the latter's travels. Auntie, on the other hand, took every chance to speak well of Dariush's character and wealth and tried to plan the family parties in a way to ensure the presence of him and his family. Ramzi seemed quite content with this as well. The unpleasant memories were beginning to fade and things were slowly returning to normal.

A few months after Manijheh's arrival from Kashan, Salar decided to leave Mr. Ramzi's orchard. He no longer felt he belonged there. Since her return, Manijheh had only faced him by chance or at family gatherings and each time had said nothing but a simple hello. Soodabeh was away most of the time on travel, but when she was home, she also avoided Salar. Given his immense love for these girls and their brother and all the time he had spent with them, this was agonizing for Salar. One day, catching Mr. Ramzi at home, Salar went up to him and declared his decision to leave the house.

"What are you going to do?" asked Ramzi, caught off-guard, as if he hadn't heard Salar correctly.

"I want to leave here. I'm going to Kaveh's farmhouse."

Ramzi looked over at Auntie and then turned to Salar again. "Our lives would be turned upside down without you." His voice was barely audible.

Salar had his head down. "No, sir. Life goes on." His tone was wistful, as if reminiscing over the years gone by. "It goes by fast and the memories fade. People come and go; time doesn't stand still."

Ramzi could see the determination on Salar's face but didn't want to let go of him. Desperately, he said, "So you think all those great memories; the nights and days spent together; sharing each other's happiness and sadness; all that can be forgotten?"

Salar raised his head and looked at Ramzi. "Being able to forget is a great blessing. You know how much I love all of you. But my back is broken by life's events; I can hardly sleep anymore. I want to go to Kaveh's farm and spend the remainder of what people call life somewhere else. Maybe then..."

Ramzi kept watching him despondently. He didn't want him to go; a large part of his own memories would be walking out the door if Salar left. Suddenly, as if having found a solution, he asked, "Do the kids know?"

Salar shook his head. "They're adults now. They're educated and wise; they'll learn to adapt."

Ramzi seemed to have given up. "At least let your house remain how it is. I want to go there sometimes and reminisce. Maybe you'll return someday."

Salar left the orchard that same day. Manijheh and Soodabeh weren't home and that's exactly the way he wanted it. Auntie joined Ramzi and they escorted him to the door. She poured a bowl of water on the ground after him.

....

Sun was setting on the farm when Kaveh returned to his house. He had spent the day inspecting the cattle house and then taking care of business matters in his office, a two-floor edifice adjacent to the farm where all issues pertaining to the employees were handled. This was the same building Soodabeh had spent a few nights in, and Kaveh felt as if he saw her there every time he walked in.

His car parked behind the building, he was walking toward the balcony when he suddenly ran into Salar. "Welcome, father," he exclaimed, his voice overflowed with joy. "I had been awaiting you."

He then picked up Salar's luggage and took them to the room he had prepared. After meeting Soodabeh, Kaveh knew his father would leave the Ramzi house. He understood Salar well; he knew his father couldn't see Ramzi every day and not tell him the truth.

Salar went to the room Kaveh pointed out, lay down on the bed and shut his eyes without changing his clothes.

Kaveh called out to him. "I'll get the food ready while you're resting."

He then went to the kitchen and got started. With the food on the stove, he headed to his own room to get changed.

The food was ready in an hour. Kaveh arranged the plates and went to his father's room to call him out for dinner. Salar was resting on the bed and staring at the ceiling, deep in thought.

"Food is ready," said Kaveh.

"I'm not hungry."

"If you don't come, I'll bring my food and eat it in your room."

Knowing his son is stubborn and won't give up until he agrees, Salar got up. "Alright, I'm coming…"

In the hall, Kaveh placed some food on the old man's plate. "Remember, father? Every time something terrible happened you were the one who told us, "*Whether you like it or not, life goes on. Days and nights will come and go and nothing in creation will change. Time does not stop and forgetting eventually heals the wounds.*" It was you who taught us these and many other lessons..."

"I wish I hadn't said anything," answered Salar. "I wish I hadn't insisted that you and your brother pursue higher education. That other guy supposedly went to America to finish his studies and promote scientific research, but he ended up stomping on his own honor and decency. How naive of me to talk about academic achievement. I wish I hadn't been so persistent about it."

Kaveh remained silent and said nothing. That night he barely slept. He couldn't stand to see Salar so depressed; his father had been severely traumatized. Kaveh felt very sorry for him and couldn't stop thinking about the hard life Salar had lived and how much he'd sacrificed to see his children succeed. He had never remarried after the death of his wife. Working day and night doing odd jobs and then serving as help at the Ramzi household, he had done everything in his power to provide his children with an education and turn them into productive members of society. And now he was completely disillusioned. The hurt inflicted by Farhad on the Ramzi family was immeasurable. Kaveh knew his father was humiliated before Auntie as well; she was the one who had introduced them to Ahmad Ramzi and was now left to explain this debacle to her brother.

By buying half the ownership of Ramzi's factory and saving him from bankruptcy, Kaveh had tried to repay him on behalf of his family, but now, after Farhad's affront, he could not even look Auntie in the eye. He loved her like his own mother; she had given him affection and support when he had needed them most, and he could not stand the thought of hurting her feelings. Above all, he cared about his friendship and bond with Soodabeh. He gave her every right to hate Salar and his family; Manijheh's plight had been extremely painful for her. Kaveh spent that night occupied with these thoughts. In the morning when he woke and walked to the garden, he saw his father watering the flowers.

………

The Lonely Years in Rochester

Leily had been sitting on a wood bench, across from the Statue of Liberty visible in the distance. It had been an hour since she'd left the hotel and started walking about before getting tired and taking a break here. Her children and the small hotel room had been getting on her nerves; she wanted to spend the next few hours just lurking around. Her head was spinning from all the adventures she and her family had been going through. After months of drifting from one country to another, they had finally arrived in New York two days ago.

People around her came and went frantically as boats picked up packs of tourists to take to the Statue of Liberty. From the time she had studied geography in high school she had dreamt of seeing this monument in person, and now she was sitting not too far across from it. She'd heard this statue is the symbol of a free and civilized country; that everyone here is free to live as they wish; that no one gets harassed about religion; and people can dress however they want and dance in the streets or speak their minds without fear. These are the things she had been seeking and the reasons why she abandoned her comfortable life in Iran and left for America with her husband and two children.

She recalled how upset the kids were when they sold the house and how sad they felt to leave their schoolmates behind. At the airport her mother had cried hysterically but her father had encouraged them, telling Leily the kids would have a bright future and she would also live in freedom.

She remembered how cheap they had sold their home and possessions to bring the cash to America and use it to open a "business" and live comfortably.

Deluged by these thoughts, her stare was transfixed by the magnificence of the Statue of Liberty as it sat serenely under the sunlight, surrounded by waves of water. She watched as people of all races, white, black, Asian, blond and brunette hurriedly went about their business. Engrossed in her own tangled mind, she lost track of time but suddenly remembered her plan to dine out with the children and her husband, Nader. They had only been in the city for two days. The first day had been spent resting, and this morning, Nader had gone to an area suggested by an acquaintance to buy a used car so they could drive to Rochester where Leily's brother lived.

She could have sat there in awe of that magnificent statue all day, but it was time to go. She stood up and reached for her purse by her feet. It wasn't there. Startled, she looked around and under the bench but found no trace of the bag. Their entire lives revolved around that purse. All their money except the amount Nader took for the car was in there. It was their entire life savings from Iran. She ran in different directions, searched again and again under the bench, even reached in the water fountain next to it, but the purse was nowhere to be found. She now looked pleadingly at the passerby as if to ask them if they had seen it; they just looked at her awkwardly and kept walking. Her mouth was now dry and her forehead dripped with sweat. She was overcome with dread, and her face gave it away. But people kept hurrying past her without even looking in her direction as if they were wound up toy cars. Their indifference was shocking to her.

Night fell. Leily was now paralyzed by fear. She didn't know her way around, nor could she speak the language of the people who passed by without even glancing at her. She was akin to a bird whose wings had been severed. It was complete darkness now. She sat back on the bench. Her head in her hands as she sobbed, she screamed, "Why does this have to happen? What have I done to deserve this? How am I supposed to find our hotel? My God, why does this have to happen to me?"

Suddenly she heard a voice. "Can I help you? Please don't cry," said someone speaking Farsi.

I was as if the doors of heaven had opened before her. Hearing someone speaking her own language alleviated her anxiety and lifted her spirit. Raising her head, she saw a young man with black hair and dark eyes dressed in athletic gear, looking back at her sympathetically. "They stole my purse," she said with a quivering voice. "All our money was in there. Have you seen it?"

The young man answered gently. "I personally haven't, but don't worry; I'll give you a ride wherever you need to go."

Despite her apprehension, Leily didn't have a choice; she accepted the ride. Recalling that her hotel card was in her coat pocket, she reached in and gave it to the man. On the way, she told him they had been in the city for two days and her husband has been out since that morning trying to buy a car, and that she had gotten frustrated in the room and was out trying to catch some fresh air. In turn, the young man told her about his routine of coming to the shore every afternoon and running for an hour. He also let her know her hotel was actually just two blocks away. Within minutes they were there and Leily shared the news of her misfortune with Nader.

The young man introduced himself to Nader as "Farhad", said he works at Columbia University, and offered him his business card. Once he found out Nader was an engineer as well, he expressed interest in keeping in touch. Nader thanked him profusely for his assistance to Leily.

....

The road from New York to Rochester that summer morning was scenic and picturesque. The sight of green farms and the villagers working on them was a novel experience for Leily and her family. The car Nader had bought seemed nice and brand new. The cool wind was refreshing to them all.

Kamran pointed to a few horses playing around. "I never thought there would be villages in America."

Nader laughed out loud, looking at his son through the rear view mirror. "You thought all Americans live in the capital?" he said sarcastically.

Leily quietly listened to them. Kamran now turned to her. "Well now that our money is lost how are we going to live?"

Maryam scolded him. "Don't worry sir; it'll work out somehow... He's constantly thinking about food!"

Leily tried to end the bickering. "We're going to uncle Mansoor's house; he'll help us. We'll stay at his place until your father finds a job. Thankfully we're all healthy, not disabled."

Kamran wouldn't quit. "Is uncle Mansoor's house big? Is it roomy?" he asked curiously.

"What are you worried about its size for?" answered Leily impatiently. "I'm sure it's got enough room."

"Mom, by the way, what's the name of uncle's wife?" asked Maryam.

"Katy."

"Be careful how you talk now," added Leily. "Here they call people by their first names; they don't say uncle's wife."

Kamran didn't seem to understand her. "Don't they have khaleh (mother's sister) and ammeh (father's sister) here?"

"Yes, they have everyone and everything." Leily was now irritated. "But they call people by their first names."

Nader suddenly stepped on the brake and everyone went quiet. Leily looked at him nervously. "What happened, Nader?"

Nader seemed shaken himself. "Nothing, just blacked out all the sudden," he answered apologetically.

"If you're not feeling well, I can drive."

Nader pulled over to the side of the road and parked in the allowed space. "No, I'm alright. If we just stop for a few minutes I'll get better," he said, leaning back in the driver's seat. "What are we going to do with so little money left?" he then added. "How long do you think we'll be able to stay at your brother's house?"

"Mansoor is my brother after all," answered Leily with confidence. "He won't let us live on the streets. I'm sure he can keep us in his house for a while."

Maryam interrupted her parents' conversation. "Uncle Mansoor is really kind. Every time he called Tehran, he would say really nice things to us two."

"Of course distance increases affection," said Nader with his eyes closed. "They say the farther you are, the friendlier you get." Then he tried to sound less bitter. "I'm kidding of course. Mansoor's a great guy. If he wasn't, he wouldn't have given us his address."

"If you're feeling better now let's get going," said Leily. "We still have a long drive ahead. We'll have to stop and eat too."

Nader fastened his seatbelt, grabbed a few pistachios from a bag in Leily's hand and turned on the engine. The road was starting to get foggy.

....

Embracing her brother helped Leily forget for a moment the hardships of travel and cultural isolation. He welcomed them with open arms to his small apartment. A beautiful white girl sat in front of the TV with a beer in hand. She stood and greeted them warmly, then sat back down and started watching TV again. Mansoor introduced her as Katy and said they were living together. He then brought each of them a bottle of water and asked if they'd had dinner yet. Nader told him they'd already eaten but were very tired.

Leily added, "My dear Mansoor, you have no idea what happened to us. They stole all our money in New York."

"How? Where? How much was it?" Mansoor was clearly upset.

Nader didn't allow Leily to explain and answered on his own. "It was Leily's mess. The lady here goes sightseeing in New York, gets mesmerized by the Statue of Liberty, next thing she knows they've taken her purse."

"Everything we had is gone," added Leily. "We barely made it here."

Mansoor felt sorry for her. "Unemployment is a big problem here," he said sympathetically. "A lot of people aren't doing well. Don't be so worried my sister, everything will turn out fine."

Encouraged by his words, Leily smiled. "I knew we could rely on my brother. Everyone needs support in a foreign country. Now dear Mansoor, can we stay at your house for a while until we find a place?"

He fidgeted awkwardly and looked over at Katy. "My dear Leily, as you can see, this house has only one bedroom," said Mansoor with a quivering voice.
"It's very small. Besides, I don't think Katy would agree."

Feeling like she had been punched in the face, Leily looked down. Mansoor's reply had embarrassed her thoroughly before Nader. She thought of the good Iranian traditions. Hospitality is an Iranian characteristic; how could Mansoor so bluntly turn them away?

Nader interrupted her thoughts. "Well dear Mansoor, what happened with the university? Did you get your doctorate?"

"No, I haven't had the time. I've been forced to work to support us. Occasionally when I have the money I take a class."

"Then what are you doing right now?" asked Leily with concern.

"I do carpentry, but the jobs are on a day-to-day basis. Katy has a full-time job though. She's the one paying the rent here."

Leily turned toward Katy. The girl still had her feet up on the table in front of the TV, drinking beer and staring at the screen. The volume was very high. But Katy continued to watch, indifferent to the presence of others and laughing loudly every few minutes. A sitcom seemed to be on. Kamran and Maryam were seated on the floor and watching the TV in front of them.

Leily looked at Mansoor. "Now what do we do?"

"Listen my sister, don't be upset," gently answered Mansoor. "I know an affordable hotel around here that I'll take you to. Stay there for a few days until I can find an inexpensive place for you guys. I'll also pay a week's worth of the hotel fees so you won't have too much to worry about."

Leily was still offended by Katy and her behavior. "Is Katy this way with everybody?" she asked her brother. "Is this how she shows hospitality?"

Mansoor could see the agitation on his sister's face. He tried to calm her down. "She doesn't mean anything by it; she has a good heart. Don't take it seriously."

Leily frowned. "Remember brother, this is not the way to treat a guest." Then she called out to Kamran and Maryam. "Get up and let's go."

An awkward, embarrassed smile appeared on Mansoor's face. "Don't let it get to you," said Nader, noticing his expression. "It's your sister after all. She's been out of sorts ever since our money was stolen. Everything upsets her. Don't take it to heart and don't say anything to Katy either. Now let's go to that hotel you were talking about."

·· ·· ··· ··· ·

Two weeks had now passed since Leily, Nader and the children arrived in Rochester. Mansoor helped them find a small apartment in a low-cost area. He also enrolled the kids in an English tutoring class, and found Nader a job in his own place of employment. He really helped them as much as he could. Little by little, Leily was getting used to the situation, still waiting for the realization of the dreams that prompted their move to America.

Nader worked five days a week from morning to afternoon. The first week he received his paycheck, he sat down with Leily and they calculated quickly that it wouldn't cover their expenses. She offered to start working, but he rejected the idea; he wanted her to attend to the children. "This is a foreign country," he said. "We have to keep an eye on the kids. If we both work outside the house then who's going to take care of them?"

A month passed. Nader worked tirelessly and had earned the respect of his manager. Maryam had been doing well in English class, but Kamran didn't care much for school and homework. Leily in the meantime had been trying to cut costs as much as possible; she couldn't bring herself to spend Nader's hard-earned money on trivial things. But in the second month they discovered they still have too little to even pay for rent. Mansoor, who had been checking on them every few days, understood what was going on and paid the rent for them. But Leily didn't wish to keep imposing on her brother. One night, out of the sight of the kids, she talked to Nader alone.

"Nader, I'm going to start working in a few days."

"What type of job?"

Leily could see his grim expression but went on. "I got a job at a restaurant."

"When did you do this?" He was surprised.

"Does it matter when? You're being worn out. Look at your face; you've aged so much in the last few months. I want to help you out. We have to manage this life together."

Nader held his head in his hands and squeezed hard.

"Don't act crazy," Leily said. "This isn't our homeland; we can't expect others to have our back. If we want our kids to have a better life we both have to work."

Nader seemed on the verge of tears. "I never thought my wife Leily would work in a restaurant one day."

....

Once Leily started working, their finances improved. But they saw each other very little now. Nader worked mornings to afternoons and when he got home Leily was already gone, and when she came back he would be asleep. A few months passed this way with them going through life like zombies, not knowing where they are and what they're doing.

Maryam was learning English quite well, so much so that she started handling the family's paper work and correspondence. Kamran, on the other hand, did not have much interest in academics. Nader and Leily only had enough time to simply ask the kids how they did in school, and they would always say they were doing well. This was enough for their parents.

"I need a sneaker," Kamran told his father one night. "Otherwise I can't play for the school team."

Nader had heard about the emphasis placed by American schools on athletics and extracurricular activities. "Alright, son. I'll take care of it."

He decided to borrow a little more money from Mansoor. He knew that his own income and Leily's only covered the rent, electricity and cable bills; any extra expenses would leave them short for food. The next day at work when he saw Mansoor, he almost said something but felt embarrassed. He thought it would be better if Leily asked instead, but he knew she'd resist. Then he had an idea. "By the way, how does one get a bank loan in America?" he asked his brother-in-law.

"Why do you need a loan? What kind are you looking for?"

"Like if someone needed a couple of thousand dollars, what would they have to do?"

Mansoor described the different types of financing and offered to apply for a credit card on his behalf. They could use that card for purchases and then pay off the fees in installments. Nader, surprised how easily credit could be obtained, accepted happily and asked Mansoor to do him the favor.

To learn English better, Leily had signed up for a program designed to teach English to adults. She attended class two mornings a week but Nader's work schedule did now allow him to do the same. Slowly, they got used to life in America. Those few months alone had helped them come to terms with many issues faced by immigrants.

A week later, Nader received a packet in the mail. A card and a letter were inside. Not being able to read English well, she gave the letter to Maryam when she came home. She put it down halfway through and told him with a happy smile that he'd received three thousand dollars in credit. Nader and the children were overjoyed. They stayed up until Leily returned from work, and Kamran was the first to give her the good news.

The next day Leily and the kids did a great amount of shopping. When Nader came back in the afternoon, he took the children out again to buy Kamran athletic gear and get Maryam everything she needed. That week they purchased everything they had wanted both for themselves and the house. Life in America was now a little sweeter for them. Nader thanked Mansoor for securing the credit card and told him such things aren't available in Iran. Mansoor advised him to watch their spending in the meantime.

One night after returning from work, Leily told Nader something had happened that he should know about. "What's the matter?" he asked anxiously. "Did you have an argument with your boss?"

She laughed at Nader's frightened expression. "Relax! They haven't fired me."

"I'm not worried you'll get fired. It's other things…" he replied resentfully, and then stopped himself. "Nothing. Just tell me what happened."

Leily smiled playfully. "Don't worry. You're stuck with me; I'm not going anywhere."

"Will you tell me what happened or not?" asked Nader softly, a little calmer now.

"Tonight when I got done, my manager called me into the office and talked to me for a few minutes."

Nader looked intensely curious. She added, "He told me he's very happy with my performance; he wants to give me a raise. But only if I work till twelve every night."

"He can go to hell," shouted Nader. "For a few extra cents he wants to keep a family woman at the restaurant till midnight!"

Leily interrupted him. "What's with the macho nonsense? He didn't say anything inappropriate; he only gave me an offer. I can either accept it or not. This is America. Everyone can decide for themselves."

He watched Leily with sadness, as if he finally understood what she meant. "I know this is America, my dear Leily; no one can tell anyone what to do. I know all of this. But I don't want you to work late at night. What can I do? My heart won't accept it." Nader felt irate and frustrated in the face of all these challenges. It wasn't easy to abandon the customs and traditions he had adhered to in his homeland. Resigned, he ended the conversation. "Do whatever you want."

The next day when Nader arrived at work, his boss called him in. Nervous and concerned, he entered the office, thinking there must have been a complaint. He did not want to lose his job; that would have wrecked their lives. The boss, knowing Nader's difficulties with English, called over Mansoor to interpret for him. Once he understood what the manager was saying, Nader was so elated he almost kissed the man, before Mansoor stopped him and let him know that wasn't customary here. They agreed for

Nader to stay overtime three nights a week. Euphoric, his eyes were twinkling with joy. When they left the office he stopped for a second and put his hand on Mansoor's shoulder. "I honestly don't know how to thank you. You've been like a true brother to me."

Mansoor laughed. "Because you do everything backwards."

The overtime hours meant Nader would get home late a few nights a week, but there was no alternative.

………...

When the owner of the restaurant received Leily's negative response, he fired her, saying he needed someone who could work till midnight.

Leily was once again gripped with dread and uncertainty. She didn't want to tell Nader and couldn't figure out why things didn't work out no matter how hard she tried. Cursing her luck, she tried to contact a friend she usually confided with, but the person couldn't be reached.

Suddenly her face lit up. She remembered a former co-worker telling her two weeks ago about another restaurant hiring, which she hadn't considered due to the long distance. It would be great if she could work there now. Leily called the co-worker and was told the other place still needed employees and that the friend would speak to the manager.

Fortunately that night, Nader came home late and didn't notice Leily's early arrival. She also didn't let him or the kids know about the loss of her job, not wanting to upset them.

A week passed. Her co-worker finally called and informed her she could start work in two days. Leily was ecstatic. Now that she had a new job, she told Nader about being fired and finding new employment, and also let him know that she needed a car now due to the long commute. Nader was indignant for being kept in the dark, but told her she could buy a car from one of Mansoor's friends who owned a dealership.

Two months after obtaining their credit card, they received the first bill in the mail. When Nader showed Leily the statement, he heard her exclaim fearfully. "How are we supposed to pay this off?"

Nader's mouth was dry. He went to the fridge and gulped down a bottle of water. "Nader, what are we going to do?" again asked Leily, squeezing the bill in her hand.

"I think we'll have to work twenty-four hours a day."

Leily stood frozen, looking puzzled at Nader. He saw her condition and tried to calm her down. "Well, debt is a part of life. We'll work and pay it off."

"Where are we going to work? How can all this debt be repaid?"

Nader answered even more gently. "Starting this month I'll work overtime."

"You can't pay this kind of bill with a little overtime," said Leily, still distraught. "We still have the car payment starting this month. I think I'll have to start working mornings too. But who'll look after the kids when we're both out of the house all the time?"

Nader seemed less worried than Leily. "Well what's the solution? Do you want to go back to Iran?"

"No, never," she shouted. "My children have to go to school right here and build their futures in this country. This is why we came to America to begin with."

....

Within a week, Leily was working in the mornings as well. She would leave home at nine and return around ten at night, seeing Nader only occasionally before sleep. And on the weekends if one was home, the other would be working.

A year passed. They got a few more credit cards and racked up even more debt, with the interests on each card gradually increasing.

Despite Leily working two jobs and Nader earning more from overtime, they still faced shortage every month due to the car payments and credit cards.

Days and weeks came and went with them barely seeing each other and having even less contact with their children. They would send them off to school in the mornings, and at nights when they would return from work, the kids were either asleep or in their rooms with the doors closed.

It had now been almost two years since Leily and her family arrived in America. She seemed quite worn out compared to those early days and the lines on her face indicated premature aging. She didn't take care of her appearance anymore; she simply didn't have the time. For a while now she'd felt Nader being inattentive and pulling away. He often came home late, and some nights he didn't come home at all. When he did, he would walk in the room tiptoed so as not to awaken Leily. But she could smell alcohol all night.

Life had become hellish for her. Working every day dawn to dusk, she felt like a machine. By the end of the day she was so exhausted she could barely think straight. Arriving home she would find her children stretched out in front of the television and watching movies, often so engrossed they wouldn't even answer her hellos. Already tired, she still had to cook them food, wash their clothes and do chores around the house. Sometimes the kids would eat unhealthy fast food such as Pizza, Hamburgers and so on, which made Leily quite mad. When she asked them about their studies they always assured her everything was fine, and she believed them based on their annual report cards. As time went on, even speaking Farsi was getting difficult for them!

The children were getting older and Leily could sense their attitudes becoming increasingly stranger. Kamran would wear his hair in the spikey punk style and Maryam was becoming more and more temperamental. As for the husband and wife, the only thing they did anymore was discuss their mounting debts. The cards may have helped them in some ways, but the daunting bills weighed so heavily on their minds, Nader would drink himself to sleep most nights and Leily had to rely on anti-anxiety medication. Their debts had reached a point they had to borrow from one card to pay off the other. Their lives were alarmingly dependent on the cards now. They owed so much they could hardly account for it all.

Once in a while when the chance presented itself, Leily and Nader would take the kids to restaurants. They had begun to notice the change in their children's characters; that shyness and childlike innocence was gone. This upset Leily a great deal. She saw herself missing out on watching her children grow up. Her own love life had turned cold as well, crumbling under the load of work, pressure and debt. Her forehead had developed deep wrinkles and she was perpetually tired. Kamran and Maryam constantly pestered them with different items to purchase, and when told about the lack of money, they would simply say, "Well just use the credit card" as if the card was a magical piece of plastic that money grew from like a tree! Influenced by peer pressure and competition with classmates and friends, they had crushed their parents under mountains of debt. Despite it all, Leily and Nader tried to maintain their composure, and wishing for their children to live in an advanced country, did everything to provide for them so they could become prominent and educated members of society. Was this not the very reason they had immigrated to America after all?

One Sunday everyone happened to be home. Nader asked Kamran a few math questions and the son couldn't answer.

"Don't they teach you algebra and geometry in school?" inquired Nader.

"Yes."

"So what's the answer to that question?"

"Leave me alone dad! I don't know!"

"Then how did you pass the exam?"

"We don't have failure," Kamran answered. "They pass us whether we learn or not."

Nader's eyes widened with amazement. "What does that mean? How can someone just pass for no reason? Now just answer this geography question. Surely you know this one."

Kamran couldn't answer that either. Nader now shouted. "What kind of school is this where they teach you nothing?"

"What the heck are you talking about??" said Kamran in English. "You've been here for years and still can't speak English! Now you're asking *me* what I've learned?"

Nader felt ashamed and humiliated, but swallowed his rage. Leily was flabbergasted by what she had heard. "What right do you have to speak to your father this way?" she scolded her son. "Why did you disrespect him?"

Kamran stood up angrily and left the room. Leily spent that night in a state of agitation, blaming herself for allowing work to distract her from imparting discipline to her children. But without work, how else could their lives have been managed? She held herself responsible for not knowing the lifestyle and economic system of the country she had moved to, and thus becoming entrapped in a financial situation unlike anything she'd known in her old country. In Iran everything she owned belonged to herself. Her house; her car; her furniture; all were her own property and she owed no debt on any of them. Credit cards as they exist in America were not used in Iran. Taxes were not back breaking.

While it's true that in Iran–as everywhere else---the lower classes don't have access to the luxuries of the affluent, in America these credit cards allow people to buy the things they can't afford while entangling them in a cycle of debt and liability, and even worse, a form of psychological bondage that is in many ways worse and more abhorrent than the plight of poverty and economic deprivation.

That day at work, Leily had a bad headache which grew worse through the day and was compounded with a fever. By three in the afternoon she could no longer stand it, and with her manager's permission she returned home. When she arrived around three-thirty, she heard unusual noises from Kamran's room. Taken aback, she opened the door. What she saw almost made her collapse.

Kamran along with two girls and another boy were lying around in the room, smoking hashish! The girls were half naked, lounging nexKamran and his friend. The boy, with a tattooed body, a punk hairstyle and a large earing in one ear, was clearly high. The girls were even worse, with tattoos on their thighs and stomach and piercings in their navels. They too were semiconscious from drug use. They all were startled by seeing Leily and tried to put themselves together. The boy jumped up and the girls crawled to a corner. "What's going on here?" shouted Leily, shaken and horrified.

The girls smirked while putting on their clothes, clearly still under the influence. "We're going," they told Kamran. "We'll see you later."

The punk friend put his pants on and with his eyes barely open turned to Kamran before stumbling out of the room. "Don't forget about tomorrow."

"Why did you come home so early today?" asked Kamran rudely, still lying down.

Leily lost control. She jumped on Kamran and raised her hand to slap him. But Kamran was tough and strong now. He caught her hand midair. "If you hit me, I'll call the police."

"What are you going to do?" she asked with a tone of surprise and condescension.

"I'll call the police and tell them you hit me. This country has laws; parents are not allowed to beat their children."

Leily found it hard to breath. She left Kamran and went to her room, closed the door and sat on the floor in shock. She felt nauseous and her fever was now worse. She ached all over as if she had been beaten with a hammer, but nothing hurt as much as the pain in her heart. What had just befallen her shook Leily to the core. She wanted to run away, but she didn't know what to run from: Herself? Her son? Her life? She wanted Nader there to share her pain, but where was he? Why isn't he here? Actually where is here? What is she doing in this country? She couldn't remember why she was even there. She picked up the phone and called Nader's job. A friend who worked there told her Nader hadn't shown up to work in a week. Leily was now afraid and bewildered to the point of paralysis. The world was spinning around her. She kept asking herself, "What am I doing here?" All the sudden she remembered: Oh yeah! She'd come here so her children would become educated and upstanding members of society. So that she could live in a civilized country, live in freedom and learn from Western enlightenment. She thought to herself, *"Was this that enlightened Western culture?"* Here she was less free than a slave. A culture devoid of spirituality and morality cannot be civilized; capitalism by itself does not bring about enlightenment. The economic system here had her in shackles and she couldn't see a way out.

She marveled at the way the magic box of television—one of the symbols of civilization—has enslaved the masses. They spend day and night chasing a few more dollars to the point where they lose sight of everything around.

They drive on congested streets and freeways from dawn to dusk to earn a handful more, and then spend the night watching programs packed by the self-serving producers with beguiling and enticing messages whose aim is to brainwash the viewer while offering some entertainment. The main effect of these programs is little more than promotion of deviation and decadence in the guise of fancy Hollywood productions. Was this the famous Western civilization?! Was this the reason she gave up all her blessings in Iran and endured extreme hardship to reach these deceptive spectacles? The destruction of the dignity and honor of herself and her family; the corruption of her husband and children and their disrespect to mother and father; the daily suffering; the humiliating jobs whose wages they had to hand over on a silver platter to the banks along with interest! Was this what she had been seeking? In these few years, the media and Hollywood had drilled every imaginable filth into her children's heads. There was so much sex in films it made her disgusted with all media as a whole. The more obscene the acts, the more acclaim they receive. People have been conditioned to the point where anything vulgar is perfectly acceptable.

Her son and daughter, who once sat before their parents with respect, now stretch out their legs and don't move away from the television and computer. She wished they would at least use the technology for learning and access to knowledge, but alas, that was not the case. If it was, then how come her children had become so alienated from her? Why couldn't she understand these creatures of the internet? She had even discovered that parents don't have the right to discipline their children, because the children could report them to the police!!

Leily could not stop these thoughts roaring around in her mind like tidal waves. She reflected on how she had abandoned her comfortable life and burned all bridges behind her. She considered she had left a country where freedom of speech and expression where nonexistent; where freedom of choice had no meaning and if her views offended the government she'd end up in jail. Women's rights were trampled upon and their opinions on politics and social issues were ignored; they didn't even have the right to choose their own clothing and men treated them tyrannically. She had to escape from these outrageous evils. She had to seek shelter in a place where women's rights still existed; where their views were valued; where she could protest without fearing violence and torture.

Leily thought these were the reasons for her move to America, and now was facing a disintegrating family gripped with addiction and debt, on the verge of losing their very humanity.

She sat motionless in a corner of the room, trying to rein in her chaotic thoughts. After a while she got up and took a shower. Her fever a little better but her head still throbbing, she went to bed to get some rest. She was barely able to relax before she sensed Nader coming in. He was walking on tiptoes so as not to wake her. Despite her poor condition she was still curious to know why he had left his job; she had to find out the reason.

She woke early the next morning. As they had breakfast together per usual, Leily seemed uneasy. "Why do you look sick?" asked Nader.

"I had a fever yesterday. I wasn't feeling well. Now I'm a little better."

Nader didn't inquire further. She stood, didn't see the kids and didn't ask for them, said goodbye to Nader and left the house. She spent the rest of the day anxious and stressed, feeling miserable and unable to focus at work. At noon she called Mansoor. "You're finally here my unkind brother."

Mansoor sounded surprised. "What's the matter, my sister? I was only on travel for a month."

Leily seemed strengthened now. "Well in that same month a lot of things happened that you didn't tell your sister about."

"What kind of things have I kept from you, dear Leily?"

"Nader doesn't go to work anymore. You didn't know?!"

"I found out today. It's the first day I've been at work since coming back from the trip. It seems he's changed jobs. Of course he had told me a long time ago he might do this but I didn't think he'd go through with it."

"Do you know where he works?" asked Leily.

"I don't know the location," answered Mansoor. "But I did get the phone number from his co-worker to get in touch with him."

Leily took the number and found the address by calling the location. Nader was working for a computer company. At four when she got off, she drove to Nader's work. She parked the car in the vicinity and sat there waiting for her husband. A strange feeling told her he's hiding something from her. Years of married life had taught her when men come home late they're usually up to no good.

Around five-thirty, Nader emerged from the building with a beautiful American woman and they left in his car. Stunned, Leily followed them. She still didn't know what was going on. The two parked in front of a restaurant and went in together. Leily sat in her car, dumbstruck. Her heart was racing. She was praying to God this is only a friendly meeting.

Two hours later Nader and the woman left the restaurant and took off in his car with Leily trailing them. The car turned into an alley and stopped in front of a house, the two got out holding hands and went inside. Watching this, Leily trembled as if ice water had been injected in her veins. The façade had fallen and the bitter truth was now plain before her eyes. She had no sensation left in her body; she felt dead.

She remained frozen behind the wheel for some time. Then without reacting or showing an ounce of emotion she headed home.

·········

Three days passed. Three days that were some of the darkest and most painful in Leily's life. She had to make a decision. Actually, she had already made it when she saw that scene; she just had to implement it.

One Sunday off from work, she went to see her friend, Miss Akhtar. Leily had two Iranian neighbors whom she visited whenever she had the chance. Both had sought political asylum in America after the revolution and had taken American citizenship. One of them was Miss Akhtar, a woman in her 70s. She had lost her husband a year after arriving in America, and worked in a hair salon to support herself and her mentally challenged niece who lived with her.

According to Akhtar, they had purchased a house using the money they brought from Iran in addition to a bank loan which they paid monthly along with heavy interest. She had worked nonstop for the last thirty years, to the point where her back was now bent and her legs were afflicted with arthritis, causing her difficulties with walking. And the problems didn't end there; her main concern was the mentally challenged niece living with her whose parents had perished in a car accident back in Iran. Unable to receive government benefits due to the small savings she had brought with her to the country, Akhtar worked until the age of seventy without complaints.

Leily's other neighbor and friend was Miss Parvin who was around sixty years of age and had also immigrated to America following the Iranian revolution. With her husband, they had utilized their savings to open a small restaurant and used its income to support themselves and their children. They had a son and a daughter who were both in college, had adapted to the American way of life and were happy with their circumstances. They had their differences with their parents in terms of outlooks and beliefs, but were able to pull their own weight and also succeed in academics. Miss Parvin was quite unhappy with the fact that her children could not speak Farsi well, and blamed herself for allowing work to distract her from teaching them their native language.

Leily saw these friends from time to time, and found comfort in getting together with them to share stories from the past and commiserate over each other's troubles and concerns.

That Sunday, Miss Akhtar welcomed Leily warmly but could tell from her grim expression that something was bothering her. She asked what the problem was. "My husband is cheating on me," said Leily without pretense. She was on the verge of tears.

Miss Akhtar responded sympathetically. "For a large number of Iranian men and women, the first thing they learn and act upon after settling abroad is to abandon their families and find someone else. It's almost as if this is their only reason for coming to America. Well, what are you planning to do now?"

Leily was despondent. "I don't know. We sold all our belongings in Iran and came here. Our entire savings were stolen the first few days and we've been crushed under credit card debt. To feed our children and survive, we've worked ourselves ragged day and night. Our only goal was for our children to grow up and get an education in a free and advanced society and for me to enjoy the same rights as my husband. But look where I've ended up now!"

Leily began to sob and raised her voice. "I haven't had a moment of peace from the day I set foot in this country. Now I can't even bring myself to return and face my family back home. There is nothing I can do. Nader has become a depraved alcoholic; my son smokes hashish, and my daughter who is about to finish high school is behaving wild and bizarre. And I'm so overwhelmed with two jobs and other problems I don't even have the time to sit for an hour and talk sense into her."

Miss Akhtar felt deeply sorry for Leily. Her old, gentle eyes were moist with tears. She could see that Leily was breaking and aging before her very eyes and there was nothing she could do for her. She could remember a time when Leily was fresh-faced, stylish and elegant, but lately the young woman had not been looking after herself and appeared older and more worn out with each passing day. Miss Akhtar couldn't do much other than offer consolation and be a shoulder for her to cry on.

Leily stayed with Miss Akhtar that day until sundown. When saying goodbye, the old lady embraced her warmly. "Think as though your mother is here; come any time you feel like."

A great feeling overcame Leily as she pondered how nice it is to have someone to open your heart to, and how good it is to have a friend who only wants your friendship.

············.

A week passed after Leily's meeting with Miss Akhtar. Physically and psychologically broken down, she could no longer even make simple decisions. She had become completely indifferent to life's problems. Day after day, akin to a zombie, she would wake in the morning, do some house chores, go to work, and return around ten at night. She seldom saw Nader and didn't want to see him either. The only time they spoke was when paying the monthly bills, and even then it was no more than a few sentences.

Nader didn't come home most nights. And Leily did not question him either. She didn't even tell Mansoor about Nader's infidelity; she believed he would only try to mediate when in her mind Nader was already dead.

She now only thought of her children. She wanted to send them to college by any means possible even if it meant the destruction of her own life. She was willing to give up everything just so her kids could have a bright future. Their unruly conduct, their lack of respect for her, and coming home some nights even later than her, all those were tolerable as long as she could see them advance in this new country.

But life seemed to have even more hardship in store. Recently Leily had noticed Maryam, eighteen now, gaining weight rapidly and looking pale and lethargic. She had thought about taking her for a medical checkup, but hadn't had the chance and kept putting it off for tomorrow. That day Miss Parvin dropped by for one of her occasional visits, bringing some food from her family restaurant. Leily was quite happy to see her, but noticed the look of concern and distress on her face. "Let's sit in the kitchen and have some coffee together," said Leily, taking the plate of food.

Miss Parvin sat down in the kitchen. "I'm here to tell you something," she said abruptly. "But I don't know how to say it!"

Leily was alarmed by Miss Parvin's tone and demeanor. "What is it? Say it already! My heart is jumping out of my chest."

"If you act this way, I won't say it at all."

"Fine, I'm calm. Tell me what happened."

"I saw Maryam today in a store. She was sick and looked pale. When I asked her about it, she broke down and said she's pregnant, has been for five months and you don't know."

Leily's legs were shaking. Her head was spinning. She sat down. Her eyes looked dead.

Miss Parvin quickly brought a glass of water and made her drink. Leily's hands trembled. Panicking, her friend tried to calm her down. "It's not like it's the end of the world; we can help her... We'll find the father of the child and we'll force him to marry her!"

Leily was speechless. With all her problems this was the last thing she needed! Miss Parvin was flustered by Leily's condition. "Try to compose yourself," she told her shaken friend. "You have to help her out."

"How?" Leily sounded desperate.

"Talk to her. See who the father is... We'll just sit here till she comes home."

"She comes late at night. I used to think she's studying with her friends."

Leily then put her head in her hands. Miss Parvin sat there for a while and tried to comfort Leily till it got late and she had to leave. Kamran was watching movies in his room. Leily continued to sit in her chair, immobile and unresponsive, akin to a lifeless creature. She blamed herself for this calamity and cried inside at her negligence and inattention. To find what she thought was freedom she had given up all her possessions in Iran, but here she had lost things even more valuable: her husband; her youth; her daughter's innocence. Now she felt what she had been seeking was nothing more than a mirage: the mirage of freedom!

Leily was angry and could not think objectively in this condition. In effect she was overlooking the good features and focusing only on the bad aspects of this country, but the fact remained that her current life was not what she had come here for, as even her dignity and self-worth were now on the verge of eradication. Leily believed it was the injustice and violation of human rights in undeveloped countries that compelled their citizens to flee to America, in the hopes of living under a fair and modern legal system.

She had learned from a television documentary about human-trafficking cartels in Thailand which make children blind, train and send them to the streets for begging during the day, then gather them in a safe house every night to collect the money. She also knew about the practice of circumcising young girls in parts of Africa and selling them to men as sex slaves. These were the types of evils the oppressed masses in undeveloped countries sought shelter from under a just and lawful system in America.

Leily was well aware that most of those who come to this country do so for the liberties found here, but it pained her to see that this haven for the downtrodden and freedom-seeking is also decaying. This was a tremendous psychological blow.

It was around eleven at night when Maryam came home. Seeing her mother seated by herself in the unlit kitchen, she came and sat next to her without turning on the light. Her voice was quivering. "What should I do now?"

"Who is the father?" asked Leily in a calm tone. Her voice sounded unfamiliar to herself.

Maryam was despondent. "A married man with kids. He left."

Leily kept listening, waiting for more details.

"We were at a party... everyone was drunk and half-conscious... I didn't know what was going on!"

"Were you on drugs?"

Maryam simply put her head down without responding; she didn't want to feel more humiliated. Leily didn't wait for the answer. She stood, filled up a glass of water and went to her room. Locking the door, she lay on the bed and stared at the ceiling. She was numb, tormented by the knowledge there was nothing she could do.

Around midnight Nader came home. He tried to enter the bedroom but the door was locked! After knocking a couple of times without a response from Leily, he threw himself on the sofa across from the television and passed out. He was heavily intoxicated!!

The next morning Leily phoned her place of work and took the day off. With Nader still asleep on the sofa, she skipped breakfast, got dressed and left the house with Maryam. It took half the day to find a doctor and discover that Maryam is five-months pregnant and not even able to have an abortion. The baby had to be kept. They returned home around dusk. Leily warned Maryam. "Either you find the father and work something out, or you'll look for a job and when your baby is born I'll help you with raising it. That's all!"

She then went to her room, put on a pair of jeans and a T-shirt and left the house. She didn't feel well. She was sick of everything. She wanted to talk to someone; just talk and have that person listen. She thought of Miss Akhtar and headed to her house.

Miss Akhtar was in the kitchen. When the bell rang, she stopped cooking and walked to the door. Her legs hurt. The joints in her hands were severely inflamed from working and using the blow dryer at the salon. She had a wristband on her right forearm and her expression was indicative of physical pain. Opening the door and seeing Leily, she took a step back and forgot her own pain. The young woman's face seemed to have aged a hundred years.

Leily's eyes were dim and she shook all over. Miss Akhtar took her by the hand and led her inside, sat her on the couch and brought her some hot tea from the kitchen. Her hands trembling, Leily cried silently as she drank the tea. These were tears for years of alienation, for the death of her hopes and dreams. They were tears for her wretched life.

Miss Akhtar embraced her. With Leily's head on her shoulder she caressed her hair like a loving mother.

"Maryam's pregnant," said Leily amidst the sobs.

Miss Akhtar was startled. But her wisdom and life experience helped her compose herself.

"It's not the end of the world," she said, holding Leily tightly. "I'll help you. I'll take care of the baby."

Leily continued to cry. "I pray that you're never taken from me, but I can't expect you to take care of a baby with all this pain and damaged wrists. I don't know what I should do."

"Don't worry about my pain. It hurts more to see you suffering so much away from the homeland. Have you told her father?"

Leily was now seated across from Miss Akhtar and felt a bit calmer. "I want to get a divorce," she said. "I've been thinking when the baby is born we'll return to Iran."

Being more experienced and also more knowledgeable about the host country, the elder lady began talking to Leily. They spoke for quite some time. "Maryam is a victim of this society," said Miss Akhtar, feeling deeply sorry. "A society where negative values are presented as positive will surely create many victims. When drug use and casual sex are considered a virtue and avoiding them a sign of backwardness, how can you expect your child to care about education and knowledge and spend time studying and learning?"

Leily had stopped crying now. "What I can't understand is that in a country that is the greatest world power and ahead of others in all areas, students aren't taught in schools how to look out for themselves. Why don't they point out these dangers to them?"

Miss Akhtar smirked at Leily's naivete. "Some of the teachers and educators are suspect themselves. With no inkling of wisdom or character and values, they evade the responsibility of conveying moral principles to their pupils, unlike what is customary in the Eastern nations. Your poor Maryam has fallen victim to this corrupt and morally bankrupt society."

Miss Akhtar's words and her sweet, gentle manner helped Leily relax a little. She drank the tea and answered Akhtar's questions, informing her that Maryam had become pregnant after getting drunk at a party and being taken advantage of by a married man.

"That piece of filth." Miss Akhtar's reply revealed her disgust.

Seeing Leily's poor condition, she asked her to lie down on the couch and get some rest. Leily quickly fell asleep and Miss Akhtar put a blanket over her.

....

Allow Me to Love You

As an architect, Soodabeh had recently signed on to help build a township in Shiraz and was at work there along with a team of engineers. This job had been arranged for her by Kyan, whom she'd met at a seminar in the same city.

On a summer afternoon at the end of the seminar, she had visited the Hafez mausoleum. Alone in a large crowd, she stood in a corner taking in the sight when a boy selling Hafez divinations approached and asked her to buy a card. She glanced at his sweet face. "Alright, give me that second one."

When the boy was paid and left, she opened the envelope. This whole time, a tall, attractive young man had been watching her from a distance. Soodabeh noticed him as she looked up. He walked toward her. "You don't want to read your fortune?"

Soodabeh looked down at the card. It read, *'The lost Yousef will return to Kanan; worry not...'*

She laughed. The young man smiled. "Well, I guess that settled the question. Now let's celebrate the good omen and have some of Shiraz's incredible Faloodeh at that shop across the street."

"Let's go!" said Soodabeh reflexively, impressed by his confidence.

Once seated at the table, the young man introduced himself. "I am Kyan Abedi. I'm an engineer. I saw you at the seminar and was looking for an opportunity to meet you."

"I'm Soodabeh Ramzi and I'm glad to have met you." She was amazed by his boldness.

Kyan smiled. "What did you think of this year's seminar?"

"It was much better planned than previous years."

"I'm glad to hear it!"

"You were worried about my approval?" asked Soodabeh, with a smile that showed off her two dimples and accentuated her beauty.

"I was in charge of everything this year and your opinion matters to me," he answered.

"Do you work for the government?"

"Well... more or less... " he replied. "Where do you work?"

"I have a contract with a private company in Isfahan that is about to end. I'm looking for a new job."

"Where I work the government grants a lot of contracts to qualified engineers," explained Kyan. "I'll give you my card; if you wish, when you return to Tehran pay me a visit. I might have a job for you."

They sat and chatted for a while, then said goodbye after finishing their faloodeh. Kyan, a devout Muslim, had liked Soodabeh from the first glance, but didn't want to get emotionally attached since her style and attire were not very conservative. She wore a short, tight manto over a tighter pair of jeans, and her reddish pink scarf covered very little of her hair. But still, Kyan could not erase her beautiful face from his memory.

The day following the end of the seminar, Soodabeh returned to Tehran. She did not stop in Isfahan and didn't see Kaveh either. After two weeks she decided to contact Kyan. She could tell on the phone that he was delighted to hear from her. She said, "If you still have a job for me, I'd like to bring my documents for you to review." He invited her to his office at three in the afternoon the next day so they could talk.

When she arrived, a few people were in the waiting room. She approached the secretary. "Please tell Mr. Kyan that Soodabeh Ramzi is here to see him."

The secretary pointed to one of the chairs. "Please have a seat till it's your turn."

Seated near the door, Soodabeh waited for a half hour before she thought to herself, "It was pointless for me to come here. There doesn't seem to be a job for me." She stood and handed her business card to the secretary. "Please give this to the engineer. If he can't see me now, I'll come back some other time."

The secretary picked up the phone and called engineer Abedi. "Ms. Soodabeh Ramzi is here. She says she does not have time to wait; she wants to come back another day."

Before the secretary could put the phone down, the door opened and Kyan appeared, asking Soodabeh to come in. The office was a large room containing a black desk, maroon leather chairs and several computers. A round conference table was in one corner of the room and a painting depicting the Iran-Iraq war was on the wall. Seeing the picture gave Soodabeh the impression that Kyan is a genuine believer in the Islamic Republic of Iran. At Kyan's invitation, she sat on one of the leather chairs and he took a seat next to her. He had a delighted expression and seemed quite happy to see her. Wearing a brown suit and white shirt, his attractive appearance impressed Soodabeh. "Well, I'm at your service," he told her with a pleasant smile.

"I'm here for a job," said Soodabeh after a brief pause.

"I've already set it up," he immediately answered. "You can start tomorrow. The government is building a township in Shiraz and I'm the project manager."

"How much are you paying?" she inquired, placing her papers on the table.

"A lot!" He added with a serious tone, "I'll send you the contract within a week."

Soodabeh rose from her seat, handed him her cell phone number and said goodbye. A week later the contract arrived and a few days after signing and returning it, she began work.

From then on, she and Kyan saw and worked with each other on a daily basis. He was a disciplined and morally upright person, never breaking his commitments and always following through on decisions. Informed and knowledgeable, he was able to converse about any topic ranging from poetry to philosophy, music and even politics. His words resonated with her and Soodabeh learned a lot from him.

Soodabeh was a reserved and introverted girl, not prone to share her feelings with others. This concerned Kyan; he wished she would open up more and talk to him about her emotions, and even more importantly, her past. But she rarely spoke about herself and her background.

One night they went out to dinner to one of Darband's traditional restaurants. The weather was pleasant and a mild breeze blew by. They sat together on a bench covered with a few cushions and a flower-patterned kilim. Soodabeh leaned back on one of the cushions. Next to her, Kyan rested his head on his hands and stared at the sky. "I've been too consumed with everyday banalities and trivial matters. It's only moments like this that give me some peace." She glanced at him with interest. He continued. "The world can only be assessed through love." He turned to Soodabeh. "You still haven't told me if you've ever been in love."

She put her head down. Kyan gave her a sharp look. "Have you?" He needed to get an answer that night.

"I've been in love, but it was futile," she said calmly:

"Do you think you can love someone again?"

"I don't know. I'll try…"

Kyan smiled. "You gave me hope."

"I don't know. I really don't know..."

And she truly didn't know what she wanted. A vague uneasiness burdened her mind. Her entire being was consumed with yearning, but she didn't know who to direct it to. Suddenly a spark flashed in her mind – she found her answer and the way to get to it as well! She told Kyan, "Next time we go to Shiraz, when coming back I want to introduce you to Kaveh."

Hearing this surprised Kyan. She had mentioned Kaveh many times before during their trips from Shiraz to Tehran.

Soodabeh hadn't even passed by Kaveh's farm in a long time. Since the township project had finished, she'd been so busy in Shiraz she hadn't visited Kaveh once.

Kyan searched in his head for the reason behind Soodabeh's suggestion. He sensed this meeting must be important otherwise she wouldn't have excitedly brought it up all the sudden; perhaps this could even be related to his own relationship with her. "I'm going out of town tomorrow to see my sister," said Kyan at the end of the date. "I'll be gone for a week. I'll call you when I come back, but remember next Friday is my birthday."

Soodabeh laughed. "I'm sure you plan on having a party too. How old are you going to be anyway?"

"You'll find out that night. How can one not have a birthday party in the first year of knowing you?"

"Then tell me the location of the party over the phone," said Soodabeh, still laughing. "You'll probably have a lot of guests too."

Kyan again answered cryptically. "You'll find out that night."

....

In the few days Kyan was away, Soodabeh had a chance to think about herself, her relationship with Kyan and that delightful attraction to Kaveh. She didn't know what to do about it all.

Although she was a gracious, dignified and sociable woman, she did not have a close friend to confide and share her problems with. This may have stemmed from her independent streak and self-reliance. But instead she had Auntie as a mother-figure always willing to listen and be there for her; this is why she told her about Kyan.

Listening to her with great interest, Auntie could tell that Kyan has a deep affection for Soodabeh and he wants this romance to end in marriage. Sensing that Soodabeh is undecided and ambivalent, she tried to give her some emotional support and lead her toward a sound decision, but she blurted out, "What about Kaveh then?"

Soodabeh seemed flustered. "But I wasn't talking about him."

"I didn't mean anything by it. I was just saying," exclaimed Auntie in a panic.

They both looked at each other awkwardly, knowing exactly what their words meant.

A week later, on the date they had talked about, Kyan came personally to pick up Soodabeh. They went to an upscale restaurant in northern Tehran and the waiter led them to a two-person table reserved by Kyan. A vase full of roses and a burning candle enhancing the ambiance sat on the elegant white tablecloth. "Where are the rest of the guests?" asked Soodabeh sarcastically. "You said all of Tehran would be at your party tonight."

Kyan pointed at her. "Who needs all of Tehran? The entire world is my guest tonight; aren't you here?"

Soodabeh said nothing and simply locked eyes with him.

He went on. "When you look at me, I feel like a bird that knows it's flying into the hunter's trap but keeps going anyway." He then pointed to the candle on the table. "Watch this candle melting drop by drop. Our lives as humans pass the same way moment by moment and lead to nothingness. Let's savor these moments and live in the present."

Soodabeh took a gift-wrapped package out of her bag and gave him. "Forgive me if I couldn't find something worthy of you. This is only to let you know you mean a lot to me."

Hearing this made Kyan feel warm inside. He thought after all the exchanges and all the talks, he's finally captured Soodabeh's heart.

………………..

You Must Come to My Wedding

It was a cold winter afternoon. Reading the paper in his room, Salar could hear the wind blowing outside while the samovar rumbled and blew out steam in the corner. Kaveh hadn't come home the night before; he was gone on business and expected to be back in the morning. When Salar heard a car park in front of the balcony, he thought Kaveh had returned. As he went to greet him, suddenly Manijheh appeared at the door. She wore a winter coat with a wool scarf wrapped around her head and neck. Her face was red from the cold and her pretty green eyes sparkled. His heart sank at seeing her; he had missed her terribly. It had been too long since they had talked and his great wish was to see her again.

She stood right there. They looked at each other for a little while. "You just left me and took off?" she said with a resentful tone.

"You told me to leave yourself," answered Salar, grinning from ear to ear.

"I may have said it," she replied in a playful manner. "Why did you have to do it?"

She walked toward him and opened her arms. Salar went forward and kissed her forehead and they sat facing each other. Just like in the old days at Mr. Ramzi's house. "Will you make me some tea, papa Salar? I've been craving those teas you make."

Her cheerful expression delighted him. "How did you drive all this way in this frosty weather?" he asked while pouring a cup of tea.

"I came to give you the good news first."

"What news? Say it quickly."

"I finally accepted Dariush's marriage proposal. He wouldn't leave me alone for years. I finally told him everything; I wanted him to know all that had happened to me so maybe he would back off. But he said it doesn't matter to him and that he loves me and will never marry anyone else! In the end he persisted to the point that I finally gave in."

Salar took her hand. "You did well, my daughter. Dariush is a good man."

"We're getting married in the summer. I would love for you to arrange the whole ceremony."

"I'll definitely be there."

After a long period, Salar was finally feeling at peace and laughing wholeheartedly. He brought Manijheh some sweets and she told him stories from here and there, adding, "Auntie has been moody ever since you left. I think she misses you." Pausing for a few seconds, she looked intently at Salar. "I had no idea how much I love you until you left. I didn't know what a blessing it is to have you in my life."

Salar could not hear her. He was simply watching her jubilant expression and thinking to himself, *"Thank God she finally forgot about him... She's managed to put that catastrophe behind her once and for all."*

It was already dark when Kaveh returned. Seeing Manijheh stunned him. Always happy to see her, he welcomed her warmly that day as well. In a way he considered her a keepsake from Farhad. Sensitive and emotional by nature, he hadn't been feeling well lately; a suppressed sadness tormented him. He asked about Ramzi and Farshid but made no mention of Soodabeh.

Salar, who had noticed this, made a point to ask Manijheh, "How is Soodabeh doing? It's been a long time since she called me or stopped by here."

"She's met a young, rich, handsome engineer named Kyan," answered Manijheh with a mischievous tone. "They spend most of their time together."

Kaveh's expression was frozen. "Does she plan to marry him?" Salar asked her while keeping an eye on his son.

"It seems that way... definitely... you know how Soodabeh is; no one can figure out what's in her head. But she's signed a contract for a large government project in Shiraz and is working with the same young engineer. They've been working a few months now."

"Well, thank God she's keeping busy and productive," said Salar. "Now I know why she doesn't visit me."

Kaveh pretended to leaf through his notebook, but was listening intently to Manijheh. His stomach was churning. Was Soodabeh about to walk out of his life? Her lovely gaze, her words scented with romance... that starry night on the balcony together discussing love, passion and the glory of creation... was it really all over?

He could no longer hear his father's conversation with Manijheh. He felt as if he was no longer there. He was taken back to the day he parked his car on Tehran's Gandhi Street across from the crowded shops. He was there to meet one of the city's important merchants to discuss exporting some of his factory's products to Malaysia. Every once in a while when visiting Ahmad Ramzi and Farshid in Tehran, he would set up meetings with major clients and attend to the factory's administrative affairs. By now Kaveh was well known within Tehran's trade circles. During these trips Ahmad Ramzi treated him with utmost respect, because ever since Kaveh had bailed him out, the factory had not only returned from the brink of bankruptcy but had also undergone a complete turnaround and now sold out its products through pre-order. This was very gratifying to Kaveh, knowing he's been able to repay Ahmad Ramzi on behalf of himself and his family.

From the car's front window, he watched the sidewalk to his left as the crowd walked by. He had always enjoyed watching the shop windows; he would have left the car and done it now if he had the time. But suddenly he saw Soodabeh walking out of a store alongside a tall, handsome young man. Kaveh was frozen behind the wheel, unable to avert his eyes. The man took out a gift-wrapped package from a shopping bag and opened it right outside the store, revealing a colorful scarf dancing in the wind as he held it toward Soodabeh. Kaveh felt as if it was his own heart quivering in all directions. Seductively and with a sweet smile, Soodabeh took the scarf from the young man.

A sudden knock on the side window jolted Kaveh. As the merchant there to meet him got in the car and they drove away, he could still see the couple standing outside the store in the rear view mirror.

Salar's voice snapped him out of his thoughts. "Kaveh, Moosa called to say his wife has cooked dinner in honor of our guest. He's bringing it over."

Kaveh composed himself. "Why did they bother? We could have prepared something ourselves."

"Thanks to Mr. Moosa, I'll miss out on Kaveh's cooking yet again," Manijheh told Salar.

Salar smiled meaningfully. "You never know, it might happen one day."

Kaveh went to the kitchen and brought out the plates and the floor spread. At dinner, Manijheh suddenly asked him amidst the conversation, "With all your wealth, why do you live like this?"

"What's wrong with my life?" He laughed out loud.

"You don't take advantage of your money."

"I haven't had the need," answered Kaveh, still laughing. "When it's necessary I'll definitely make use of it."

Salar took a peek at him; he knew something was hurting Kaveh inside.

Manijheh spent the night there and left for Tehran the next morning. A few months later she married Dariush. Salar went to Tehran a month before the ceremony at the invitation of her and Ahmad Ramzi. His return to her father's plantation and the opportunity to enjoy his company for an entire month was wonderful for Manijheh.

Salar and Auntie took care of everything pertaining to the wedding. The ceremony was held at Ramzi's enchanting garden. Round tables covered with white tablecloth and bedecked with Magnolias encircled the pool; colorful lamps were hung among the trees... the garden was decorated in the best manner possible.

In her white bridal gown Manijheh's striking beauty shined among the attendees, and the handsome Dariush looked more distinguished than ever in his stylish groom attire. All friends and family as well as several notables of Tehran were among the guests. The music never stopped. At the nuptials, Salar presented the bride and groom with a valuable gift on behalf of himself and Kaveh, who had made up an excuse and not attended. The joy and happiness that had left long ago once again returned to enrich the lives of Ahmad Ramzi and his children. Following the wedding, Manijheh and Dariush left for France for their honeymoon.

You again, the Ones I Love

Farhad was carefully reading a letter sent from Tehran University, inviting him to attend a conference on magnetic physics. He accepted happily since not only did the subject matter interest him, he would also get to visit his father, brother and extended family.

He hadn't heard from them in a long time. Burdened by shame over his betrayal and abandonment of Manijheh and her family, he did not even have the courage to contact his father! On the other hand, the absence of phone calls and correspondence from his father and other relatives indicated a lack of willingness on their parts to be in contact with him as well. Since marrying Laura, he had been so consumed with life and personal issues in America that he sometimes forgot he even has family on the other side of the world. The few occasions he was reminded of Iran and his family often passed very quickly. Perhaps it was intentional?!

In the few years since being hired at Princeton, his achievements had helped establish Farhad as one of the chief scientists at the university and this in turn had raised his profile as a prominent scholar in academic circles worldwide.

Despite his heavy workload, he spent his free time playing golf and tennis with Laura or in the company of mutual friends and colleagues. Everywhere he went he was respected and admired; his company was sought by all. Lately he had been traveling to conferences in various American states as well as Europe and Asia and his name was being mentioned among the elite in his field in various papers and journals. He had come to America to attain his goal, and he had done exactly that.

Farhad liked and respected America as a free and advanced country where the citizens regardless of ethnicity enjoy liberty and equality. Although this freedom sometimes bordered on anarchy, it still didn't nullify the equal civil and social rights of individuals. Despite that, Farhad believed that certain limits must exist to prevent the degeneration of society since unlimited freedom has the potential to undermine the pillars of family and morality.

Farhad's appreciation and respect for the American system of governance was based on its democratic nature. He knew that the US constitution, written 220 years ago and not changed since, is a solid and ageless document that is a source of pride as a national legacy for the American people, providing them a legal framework according to which all are granted equal rights.

After years in America, he had grown used to many different attributes of the society and people in general. Still, when daydreaming, he wished he could return to a random place in Tehran just to listen to the commotion of the crowd, watch the buses traveling with the passengers at times hanging on the outside, or stare at the face of the old porter about to crumble under the weight on his back. Each of these scenes carried great meaning and emotional resonance. These thoughts crept into his mind from time to time and overwhelmed him with sorrow and nostalgia.

Since receiving the invitation from Tehran University, Farhad's grief and introversion had intensified. The arrival of this letter had been akin to a key opening the door to distant memories, leaving him restless and perturbed. He wished to fly instantly to Iran but at the same time could not face his family. He had no idea what their reaction was going to be.

He recalled the last time he had been in Manijheh's loving embrace, the worn but beaming face of his old father, and Kaveh's words in their last meeting urging him, *"No matter where you are, don't forget decency and moral principles."*

These thoughts lashed at his spirit and weighed on his heart. He missed Iran terribly; the country whose civilization dates back thousands of years. But what provoked his emotions more than anything were the good people of his country, their loyalty and kindness, the ancient Norooz, the Yalda night, and above all, the human rights cylinder of Cyrus the Great which is the template for such rights in the modern world. How could he forget all these? Are such gifts even forgettable?

Farhad thought to himself that years had now passed since his transgression against Manijheh and the Ramzi family; he hoped the passage of time had alleviated their bitterness and resentment. Moreover, his current prominence in the ranks of scholars and scientists gave him the courage to face his family again.

A few days after confirming his attendance at the Tehran conference he phoned his father. Soodabeh picked up. She immediately recognized his voice when he said hello, but did not respond.

"Can I speak to Salar?"

"Salar no longer lives here," said Soodabeh harshly before hanging up.

 Farhad was stunned. Salar never wanted to live anywhere other than the Ramzi house. He hadn't even moved to the house Kaveh had purchased for him. Getting nervous, he picked up the phone again and called Kaveh. While waiting for an answer, he reassured himself. "What am I afraid of? Manijheh and I were once lovers and then separated and went our own way. That's not a cardinal sin." Kaveh answered the phone. Hearing his voice, Farhad was so elated his voice began to quiver. "Kaveh... it's me... Farhad."

"How are you, scholar?"

"I'm fine," said Farhad hastily, feeling energized. "My only worry is your absence. I work at Princeton University. I've been invited to attend a conference in Tehran."

"I'm glad!" replied Kaveh.

"Why doesn't father live in the Ramzi house anymore?"

"Father is here with me."

"Why did he leave the Ramzi house?"

After a brief pause, Kaveh answered. "He was too embarrassed to look Ramzi in the eye... he was disgraced."

"For what?" asked Farhad. "Salar and disgrace?!"

"Yes. His son impregnated Ramzi's daughter and then went off to America and married someone else. Ramzi's daughter ended up getting into an accident and lost the five-month-old fetus that was Salar's grandchild."

Farhad's hands trembled. His legs shook. His heart was racing. He could see himself dead, yet somehow able to hear and talk. He then heard Kaveh's calm voice. "I feel sorry for you! I truly am sorry that you have to carry this burden for the rest of your life."

Farhad hung up, feeling dizzy. The world was spinning around him. He could see Manijheh's beautiful face staring at him disdainfully and saying, *"You see how you killed your child? You see how you broke my heart? I told you that you'd leave and forget me. You see how you did forget me?"* He felt extremely weak.

When Laura came home, she saw him lying on the sofa in front of the television. She could tell he wasn't feeling well. His eyes were cold and lifeless; his usual smile had disappeared. His face seemed years older. Laura was genuinely frightened. "What happened, Farhad?" she asked, anxious and worried. "Are you sick?"

Farhad didn't reply, as if he hadn't heard or seen her. Laura came and sat by him on the floor and held his hands, feeling how cold they were. "Has something happened?" she asked again.

Farhad looked at her bleakly. "My father is sick."

"Who told you?"

Farhad's voice sounded muffled. "I called to tell my father and brother about the conference and my trip to Tehran; I found out the story."

"What is his illness?"

"There is a problem with his heart," said Kaveh. He added under his breath, "I broke it."

... ...

The Burgeoning of Hope

Leily's divorce from Nader took six months to complete and he left the house around the time Maryam's daughter was born. After the birth, Leily worked and Maryam took care of the baby. Kamran was now in the last year of high school. He worked part-time in a pizza shop for pocket money and also to save for college.

One day Leily was home babysitting as Maryam ran errands outside. While singing lullabies for the baby at bedtime, she laid her head on the bed and fell asleep as well.

Suddenly she felt a hand stroking her hair. Opening her eyes, she saw Kamran standing over her. He had changed a lot since Maryam became pregnant. With his father out of their lives, he felt a new sense of responsibility. Waking early every morning, he would go to school and upon returning would busy himself with studying and helping out around the house. He had severed ties with his old friends as well. It seemed he had become a mature family man ready to take care of the household.

Leily raised her head and looked affectionately at him. He had tears in his eyes. He held his mother and gave her a kiss. "I promise to fulfill your dreams," he said while crying, looking in her loving eyes. "I have to repay you for all your efforts. I will keep going to school and I bet I'll be successful. I applied to all colleges and thankfully Columbia accepted me. I'll pay for some of the tuition through work, and the rest I can get from education loans. I want to become a lawyer. I must see you truly happy and content just one more time like you were when we first came here. We'll take care of my sister and her baby together as well."

As she listened to him, Leily cried. But these were tears of joy. Hope was beginning to take root in her heart. At least one of her wishes was coming true.

She had lost everything in search of freedom in this country – her husband; her youth; her daughter's innocence... But at this moment she found a glimmer of hope in her heart. "I need to go to Iran and borrow some money from my father," she told Kamran. "We'll move to New York and live there until you finish your education."

....

On Tehran Streets without You

Farhad booked his trip through Lufthansa airways. On a stop in Frankfurt airport, he encountered a woman that looked familiar. The lady had noticed him too; it seemed they had met each other before. She recalled who he was first and approached him. "You don't remember me? ... New York, across from the Statue of Liberty, where they stole my money ... You helped me out."

Farhad suddenly remembered. "You look very different," he said, looking at her face.

"I've aged a lot... "

"Are you traveling alone?"

"Yes," she replied, adding, "I was planning to call you. Remember giving me your number and saying you work at Columbia? I need your assistance again."

"What kind of help?" asked Farhad eagerly.

"My son has been accepted at Columbia," said a cheerful Leily, encouraged by his pleasant tone. "We plan on moving to New York when I return from Iran. With your permission, I want to send him to you for guidance."

"I work in Princeton now. But I do know people at Columbia and I'll certainly help him."

Thanking him profusely, Leily made him promise to get in touch upon returning to America and then gave him her cell phone number.

At the airport in Tehran Farhad watched Leily's relatives greeting her with bouquets of flowers. But no one was there to welcome him. Hailing a cab, he asked to be taken to a hotel and the driver took him to one of the best in the city. He spent the night there and took a flight to Isfahan the next day. Upon landing, he immediately rented a cab to Kaveh's farm.

When Farhad arrived, Kaveh was busy speaking to Moosa. Not feeling well that day, his tone was harsh and agitated. He criticized Abdol and other workers and blamed them for certain things not getting done. Moosa knew from experience that at times like this it was best not to disagree; otherwise the outcome would not be favorable.

Moosa suddenly noticed Farhad and interrupted Kaveh. "Look who's here, we have a guest!"

Kaveh turned around and rushed to embrace Farhad upon spotting him. He was genuinely happy to see his brother. "Welcome, brother," he said eagerly. "You're truly welcome. Now I realize how much I had missed you."

Farhad was tight-lipped and his expression was grim. He couldn't talk. He was at a loss for words.

"Let's go inside," said Kaveh. "Salar is resting."

Farhad entered and saw his father asleep on a mattress by the wall, his face looking old and wrinkled. Two tears rolled down Farhad's face. Taking in the scene, Kaveh became quite emotional; he felt great pity for his brother. He could see his face had aged a little; his eyes looked cold and vacant.

Gently and quiet, Farhad sat by his father's feet as Kaveh turned on the samovar.

"How is father's health?" he softly asked.

Kaveh pointed at the old man. "You can see how ragged he is. He's not the old Salar who walked around with swagger and worked several hours a day."

Farhad rested his head against the wall. His eyes red and tearful, he stared at his father's worn, callused hands. Kaveh felt deep compassion for his brother and respected his need to be left alone at that moment.

Salar opened his eyes and saw Farhad. As he tried to get up, Farhad grabbed his feet tightly, put his head on them and began sobbing.

"A man doesn't cry," Salar told him, holding back his own tears. "No one ever knows what fate has in store for them. Some things are within our control, others aren't. It's not like you even knew. What's done is done; we can't turn back the clock. I wish that was possible but it isn't. Now put yourself together. Be a man and come to terms with what's happened. Try to live the rest of your life so that such regrets can be avoided."

"I have to see her," pleaded Farhad in a weak and fragile voice.

Salar snapped. "No! Never. Forget about her. She's married and gone on with her life. Time has slowly healed the wounds afflicted by you and the world. You don't want to wreck her life all over again, do you?"

Still weeping, Farhad shook his head. "No!"

"That's the right way," said Salar paternalistically. "This is a pain that you must come to terms with somehow. Some troubles should always remain in one's heart and never shared with others. You must keep this sorrow inside."

Kaveh poured two cups of tea for them and called Moosa to pick some fruits from the garden and bring over.

He then sat next to Farhad and spoke to him affectionately; about the old times; about Mr. Ramzi's house; about how happy and cheerful he had seen him last time with Manijheh. As Kaveh talked with serenity and interest, Farhad listened with pain and regret.

....

During the three days Farhad stayed there, he told Salar about his life, his accomplishments and successes. He could see how much his father enjoyed hearing about them. Kaveh showed him the farm as well as the designs Soodabeh had drawn up for the township. Seeing all this wealth and achievement for his brother made Farhad quite happy. They went to see their uncle together, and the old man was delighted to see Farhad and was proud to have such a renowned scientist visiting him.

At the end of the three days Farhad returned to Tehran to attend the conference. During the two-day event he was met with great respect by the university officials. Once the conference ended, he stayed in Tehran. He wanted to explore the city.

For the next two days he traveled all over the city. He went by the restaurants and locations he and Manijheh used to frequent, then stopped by Mr. Ramzi's house for a few minutes and watched the walls and the gates leading to the orchard. He had so many memories from this place. Walking the streets he and Manijheh had strolled together, he had an odd feeling; it was as if she was next to him, walking alongside him.

The final night in Tehran, he stood before the house where he and Manijheh had shared their last few nights together. The tumult inside him was intense. For the next few hours he simply wandered around that area, committing the memories of this last tour to a special place in his mind.

Before his flight to New York he tried to contact Laura several times, but there was no response. He was worried, but had no choice other than to tolerate the long hours in the air to get to New York.

....

I Had Told You Not to Lie to Me

A week after Farhad left for Iran, Laura was searching for a document she couldn't find. Not seeing it where she guessed it would be, she emptied all her personal closets and shelves to no avail. The only place she hadn't searched was Farhad's room. This wasn't something she wanted to do especially since Farhad wasn't home and she saw no reason why he would keep that paper there. She went back and forth in her mind, but given her need to find the item for work tomorrow, she reluctantly went ahead and rummaged through his room.

In the first shelf she combed through, she saw a box and opened it without delay, finding several photos and a book of Hafez poetry. The pictures all featured Farhad and Manijheh in various poses, in a way which made it clear they were romantically linked.

Laura's legs trembled. She sat squatted in Farhad's room and tried to understand why he had kept these photos hidden from her. Once she regained her focus and composure, she concluded Farhad must have lied; he must still be in love with the woman whose photos he can't bring himself to get rid of.

She put the photos and book back in the box, placed it where it had been on the shelf and left Farhad's room. She thought to herself, "Now I understand why it took him a few days to answer when I first brought up marriage." Had Farhad really only married her for a Green Card and a job at Columbia University? Laura was of course aware of this, but he had also shown great affection for her since the marriage; their life together had been quite romantic. She had told him never to lie to her and he had promised over and over that they'd always tell each other the truth. Then why this?

Laura wasn't the type to allow emotions to overrule her judgment. Life with Farhad was over for her. Her mind was made up; she had to separate from him. First she considered taking all her belongings and leaving only a letter. But it was more sensible to stay until his return, discuss the matter with him and separate amicably.

....

Farhad expected to see Laura upon arriving at JFK airport in New York, but to his astonishment she was not there. He had called before the flight and left her a message detailing the times of departure and arrival as well as the flight number. But she was nowhere to be seen. Farhad of course wasn't feeling well either. His mind still preoccupied with Manijheh and the love they lost, he felt disoriented. Laura's inexplicable absence affected him even more, overwhelming him with apprehension. From the airport he called both the house and her cell phone without response.

On the way home a thousand thoughts occurred to him, but he could not make sense of anything. Laura opened the door when he arrived; her face indicated she was not in good spirits. When Farhad leaned in for a kiss she pulled away. He was puzzled. "Has something happened?"

"We need to talk," she answered without pretense.

Shaken inside, he took a seat in the living room. Laura went to his room and retrieved the box containing the photos of Farhad and Manijheh. Opening it, she placed the pictures before him. "Are you still in love with her?"

Farhad was frozen. He did not speak a word. "I'm glad you're not lying and making up stories," added Laura.

"It was a romance that ended."

Laura smirked. "I don't see that in your eyes. I always hoped after our marriage you would have that kind of love for me."

"Please forget about it," pleaded Farhad. "Let's just live our life together."

Her response was mournful. "I can't forget it; I had told you not to lie to me. The difference between us Americans and you Easterners is we don't hide our past to attain someone or get something. We may fail to get them, but we still share the truth about our background. I don't want to live with you anymore; I'd like us to separate amicably. I'm going to Washington today. When I come back, I'll go to the house I've rented."

Farhad couldn't move. He was speechless; his heart ached. Laura had been his only supporter, friend and confidant this entire time. Losing her would leave a deep void in his life. He still couldn't believe it could happen. Life would be empty and pointless without her. But he said nothing. He knew Laura had made up her mind.

He stood and faced Laura. "I didn't want things to turn out this way, for it all to end so quickly. I never betrayed you in our life together. But at the same time I can't forget my past. That's impossible; it would be impossible for anybody. Now if you can't have me this way, then I will do as you say and wish."

With tears in her eyes, Laura glanced over at him. "I thank you for your honesty. But I can't have an incomplete life. I want all of you. I want a love that only belongs to me. This is why it's better that I say goodbye."

"I'll never forget our life together," said Farhad, tears rolling down his face. "This house is always open to you; return any time you wish."

……………

Goodbye Rochester

After Leily left for Iran, Miss Akhtar felt a heavy responsibility on her shoulders. She took care of Maryam's baby three days a week, cooked for Kamran and Maryam and on some days did some chores around Leily's house. Maryam and Kamran both worked now. Kamran was happy to be accepted at Columbia University and Maryam felt good about her financial contributions by working three days at Starbucks. Her daughter was becoming sweeter and sweeter as she grew.

Miss Akhtar recently noticed a new Iranian family had moved in next door to her. Every time she found out about a new Iranian household in the residential complex, she would pay them a visit to welcome them personally. This time she did the same, showing up at the family's home one evening with a box of chocolates.

Upon meeting Miss Ozra, the lady of the house, she learned the husband's name is Reza Mohebbi. They'd lived in Rochester for a number of years and had moved into this complex only a week before.

Mr. Mohebbi had an important government post under the previous regime and had lost his job following the post-revolution purges. His family had enjoyed an affluent lifestyle in Tehran. Years ago they had sent their son Dara to America for school and he had settled in Rochester to be near their family acquaintances. In the beginning, Mr. Mohebbi sent him money every month to pay for school and life expenses. After a few years of college, Dara dropped out without explanation, turned to partying and debauchery and became a complete alcoholic. This continued until four years ago when Mr. Mohebbi faced political troubles in Iran and ended up moving to America along with his family. Thinking their son has a proper job and a dependable income after years of education, they sold all their belongings and brought the cash with them to America. Once here, they figured after a month that Dara not only has little income but has dropped out of school as well.

Mr. Mohebbi rented a house in Rochester and they settled there. They survived the first year on generous government assistance, but Mr. Mohebbi soon understood this couldn't cover all their basic needs and decided to start working. Having never had a job outside the bureaucratic world, he had no professional skills and had to rely on friends and associates to find employment. He was finally hired as a worker by a house painter. This was hard labor for him at his age, but there was no other choice. The psychological damage he endured was worse than the financial hardship.

What hurt him the most was memories of the past and the comfortable life he had left behind, knowing his status as a political refugee precluded him from returning.

He spent the first year in exile awaiting the demise of the regime in Iran. Like many other Iranian immigrants, he naively believed a coup would happen somehow and they'd be able to return happily, with everything restored to how they used to be. But he soon realized his life was going to be spent in America and that he needed to work to earn his family a livelihood.

Their first few months here saw perpetual conflict between Mr. Mohebbi and his wife. He suffered constant putdowns from her and felt humiliated before his son and daughter. Three years later their daughter was afflicted with depression which hurt him deeply. And to make things worse, he witnessed Dara going through life recklessly, working only a couple of days a week to pay for his cigarettes and alcohol.

Miss Ozra, on the other hand, had gradually lost her pomposity and self-importance, growing accustomed to a modest life. Of course she hardly had a choice in the matter. Her battles with despair and hopelessness had left their mark on her worn, doddered face.

To help out with the expenses, Miss Ozra worked three days a week at a clothing store. Selling clothes was easy for her so the job was not a burden. She was also happy to have a chance to improve her English while earning an income. On a day off from work, Miss Akhtar came for a visit. She met Dara and found him to be a tall, attractive young man with a good sense of humor. He was highly Americanized and spoke Farsi with difficulty. She took a liking to him and thought about introducing him to Maryam.

....

One day while on break at work, Dara stopped by the coffee shop nearby. Behind the counter, he noticed a new barista. Her pale, graceful face and honey brown eyes attracted his attention immediately. He could not take his eyes off of her.

"Have you just started here?" asked Dara in English when his turn came.

She smiled. "Yes, why?"

He was hoping to strike up a conversation. "The line is quite long today; it must be your pretty face drawing in the crowd."

The girl shot him a cold look and didn't respond. She then gave him his coffee quickly, took the money and called out the next customer.

Dara thought to himself, "What an arrogant girl" and tried to leave without looking at her again. The next day he came in, he didn't see the new girl. He was about to leave with his coffee when he noticed her sitting in a corner busy with a computer. Something made him approach her. "Did you quit?" he asked gently.

The girl's brown eyes turned to him with indifference. "No, it's my break time. I'm studying."

"What subject?"

"It's for college. I want to apply."

"Which college?"

The girl brushed back her luscious chestnut hair, put away her computer, and went back behind the counter without acknowledging his question. Not used to being ignored by women and accustomed to compliments and attention for his charming looks, Dara took offense to her attitude and left the shop without saying another word.

The next day at the coffee shop he noticed the girl working again, but went to another employee and completely ignored her.

....

A week after this encounter Miss Akhtar was at Mr. Mohebbi's house again to talk to Ozra, who was used to her routine visits by now. Akhtar described Leily in glowing terms and offered to host a dinner party for everyone when she returns from Iran.

On a day off from work, Dara went to the local 7-11 to buy cigarettes. He ran into the pretty barista from the coffee shop, holding a baby. "So, you live around here too?" asked Dara.

Finding it difficult to carry her shopping bag while holding her daughter, she turned to the child and said in Farsi, "Ok sweetheart, now hold yourself tight against mommy so she can carry both of you." Hearing her speak, he went toward her and took the bag. "Please let me help you," he said in Farsi. "I'm Iranian too."

Once she heard this she smiled and allowed him to carry the bag. When they exited the shop he noticed she didn't have a car. "You can't walk home with the baby and the package. My house is nearby; I can give you a ride. My name is Dara, I'm glad to meet you."

"I'm Maryam and this is my daughter Marjan," she answered before leaving, unable to ignore him any longer. "Our house is around the corner, but thanks, I'll go on my own."

Dara stopped insisting. He kept asking himself why the girl whose brown eyes had captured his heart had to have a husband.

One Sunday as he was about to leave the house, his mother told him, "Miss Akhtar has invited us over for dinner. She especially asked for you to come; make sure to return early tonight so we can go."

He resisted at first, but gave in to his mother's insistence.

…………

It was before eight when they arrived at Akhtar's house. From the noise inside it seemed a few other guests were already there. As soon as Dara entered he noticed Maryam. Initially taken aback, he composed himself and approached her, calling out, "It seems fate keeps putting us in each other's path." He then looked around to see if Maryam's husband was there. But he and his father were the only males present.

Once they sat around and tea was served, discussions warmed up; the ladies chatted together while Dara and his father watched television. When the women went in the kitchen to help Miss Akhtar, Dara took the opportunity and asked his mother where Maryam's husband was.

"She doesn't have one," said his mother, surprised by the question. "The child's father abandoned her; they weren't married."

Although this made Dara feel sorry for Maryam, deep inside he was happy to hear she's single. After dinner he sat next to her and asked about work and school.

"I have to get into college and finish my studies," said Maryam. "I want to major in computer science."

"But what will you do with your child?"

"My mother will take care of her," she answered. "Of course Miss Akhtar will help some days too." She then asked, "What do you do for a living?"

"I work at a car dealership."

"Have you finished college?"

"I only attended for three years," replied Dara. "Then I ran out of money and had to start working."

"Do you want to go to college again?" asked Maryam sympathetically.

"Of course," he said, seeming regretful. "But I can't. I don't have the patience for studying anymore."

Maryam looked in his eyes. "So you gave up."

Dara Laughed. "Well, maybe I did give up."

Maryam said nothing further and started playing with her daughter, her expression sad yet resolute at the same time. Dara suddenly noticed Leily glancing over at him disapprovingly; it seemed she hadn't liked their conversation. That night when they returned home, he had no doubt he was in love with Maryam.

From then on, Dara struck a friendship with the young woman and tried to find ways to run into her more often. One day when Maryam was on break, he stopped by the coffee shop again. Sitting at a table having coffee together, Maryam told him ecstatically, "I finally did it. I got into Columbia University. We will be moving to New York."

Dara's heart sank. "When are you leaving?" he asked pleadingly, his eyes brimming with sadness.

"Soon."

Dara realized he's about to lose everything. "Why does it all have to end so quickly?" he asked Maryam, looking her in the eye.

"A lot of times we don't value the opportunities we have," Maryam replied, maintaining eye contact. "As soon as we start getting used to something, it all ends like a game." She went on, "You're a bright, kindhearted young man. But it's a shame you're wasting your life with delusions and misconceptions, thinking you're powerless and crippled by financial problems. You're mistaken if you think you can't take advantage of the opportunities in this country. You're holding yourself back; ignoring your body and soul. The alcohol and cigarettes ravage your body and hopelessness and despair wreck your spirit. If you look well within yourself you'll see the gift God has placed in you; you'll see what I mean. There are things inside you that can guide you toward your goals, to help you find what you're looking for."

Dara sighed. "I always had an interest in the arts. All my life I wanted to build beautiful houses. I wanted to be creative."

"Go after it and you'll attain it," said Maryam. "You have to work hard for it. You know your slightest success brings joy to your parents and lessens their homesickness. You can make them happy, do you understand?"

Dara looked at her lovingly, not wanting to leave her side. He wished he could sit there for hours and talk. He wanted to embrace her.

Maryam's words had penetrated his mind. No one could have transformed his life so easily; no one else had been able to get through to him like she just did. He decided to not be the old Dara anymore.

....

Maryam and her family soon moved to New York. Leily helped her and Kamran get ready for college with the money brought over from Iran.

The day before moving, Dara went to see Maryam. The truth was she didn't want to leave him either. She was beginning to have feelings for him. "I'm sure you've gotten the sense that I love you and don't want you to leave," Dara told her that day. "But I understand you're going after your goals; I respect that. Actually I've also decided to finish my last year of college. I'll study my field of interest. I know it's very difficult and will take a long time, but I've never been more determined in my life."

Maryam felt elated. The mask was lifted and Dara's true face was now before her: strong, hopeful and driven.

It took several years for Dara to finish his engineering studies. He worked day and night but enjoyed every minute and never felt tired. Maryam kept in touch with him all the way through.

A short while after obtaining his degree, Dara secured a lucrative job in New York as an architect working for the government. He asked his parents to join him in the city, but Mr. Mohebbi rejected the idea, wishing to stay in

Rochester where he now felt comfortable and had many friends.

Maryam on the other hand was delighted to see Dara in New York. She loved him and knew she had made the right choice.

…………..

Don't Leave Me Deserted

A few months had passed since Farhad's return to New York. Laura had now left him for good. He felt her absence constantly. He understood now what a blessing it had been to have someone like her in a strange land, but there was nothing he could do other than come to terms with the circumstances. He wasn't the old Farhad anymore. Something had changed in him.

It was a spring day and he had just returned from an academic trip to Washington, D.C. The spring there is quite beautiful; the cherry blossom trees donated by the Japanese have made that city a sight to behold.

Farhad felt restless that day. To distract himself, he watched TV for a while and then went to his computer to work on a report, but could not find peace no matter how hard he tried. He turned off the computer, put on his athletic gear and went to the local gym; even exercise couldn't ease his mind. He was extremely on edge. Suddenly he thought about driving to the park across from the Statue of Liberty.

Once there, he walked around for a while and then sat on a bench facing the monument. Staring at the statue, he began to recall the hopes and dreams he had come to this country with: reaching a higher goal; solving the mysteries of physics; joining the ranks of the world's elite scientists. He had achieved them all. He now worked at one of the best universities, performed great feats in scientific research and made a name for himself as a prominent scholar. He had accomplished everything he had come here to do. Then why was he so distraught?

He felt overwhelmed with sadness. The loss of his emotional bonds and past life; burning the bridges behind him; losing Manijheh and the death of his unborn child... he was akin to someone waking from a long coma and seeing no familiar faces around. He wished to see Manijheh terribly; the same Manijheh whom he once discounted for being traditional. How he craved to be with her now, to be close to the one who had always been by his side and obliged all his wishes. He mourned as he watched his fragile love shattered at his feet, broken to pieces with a simple flick.

He felt lost without a clue where the destination led to. He now had everything he ever wanted: abundant wealth; exalted status; prominent associates... then why was his spirit flailing about in confusion and darkness? Why was he not content? Was this not the path he had insisted upon? His worldview had always revolved around electrons and atoms; he saw the mysteries of creation in terms of electromagnetics; then why was he not happy at this moment? Could it be he had erred in choosing his standards? Was it because in this vast universe, there are unknown factors whose impact on human life is no less than those elements? Was this the reason he had overlooked the basic principles of morality and compassion? Was this why he had broken a heart and hurt a soul? What is soul really?

Is soul that grand foundation of humanity which will remain the basis of all creation, all universes and all existence from the very beginning to eternity? And is soul that single and independent origin of life which if not developed can lead to human degeneration? He didn't know. He had no idea! How weak and worthless he felt in the face of this greatness. Despite all his knowledge, he felt insignificant compared to the magnificence of creation. As he stared at the Statue of Liberty, he wept silently. Yes, he was a scientist crying before the Statue of Liberty.

Night was falling and it was getting dark. He rose from the bench to get going. But suddenly as if to have found the missing piece, he remembered his encounter with Leily near the Statue of Liberty. She had given him her phone number at the airport. He gave her a call, got her address, and drove to the house.

Leily and her children were home. When Farhad was at the door he could hear them shouting and talking in Farsi; the place felt familiar to him. When Leily answered the door she noticed how much he had aged since their first encounter. She cordially invited him in. Having bought the place with the money Leily had brought from Iran, they had been living there for a while due to its proximity to Columbia. Kamran had received a university scholarship, Maryam was enrolled in college, and Leily had reduced her workload to take care of her granddaughter who was standing behind her at that moment with her cute curly locks. Farhad picked up the child and kissed her.

"Would you allow me to come here occasionally so we can reminisce about the homeland?" asked Farhad with tears in his eyes. "So I can read to you from the Shahnameh and you can read Hafez divinations for me? So we can spend Yalda nights together and celebrate the first day of Norooz?"

Leily became emotional at hearing him and seeing the tears in his eyes; his pain and sadness were familiar. She asked him to stay for dinner. "I'm cooking Iranian food tonight; will you stay?"

Farhad smiled. "I'll stay."

And from then on, Farhad visited Leily's family from time to time; taking her granddaughter out to play and spending a few hours in their company. These visits alleviated his agony and homesickness. He would also contact his father and brother once in a while to check on them. He was slowly coming to terms with his sentiments and forgetting the absence of Laura.

....

I Want to Give You the Best Wedding in the World

One Friday when Kaveh had just returned from horseback riding, he saw Soodabeh's car in front of the balcony. He felt elated; he hadn't seen her in a long time. As he got closer, he noticed her and a young man sitting together on the lounge chairs in the balcony. As soon as she saw him, Soodabeh jumped up. "This is my friend Kyan; he's an architect too. We work together. I've brought him to see the township I've designed. Of course I wanted to see you as well."

Kyan stood up and shook hands with Kaveh. "Soodabeh has talked so much about you that I had to meet you myself!"

Kaveh welcomed him in a very formal manner. His face was tired and weary. His sharp stare pierced through Kyan! "Did you see the township?" he asked his guest.

"We just arrived. I wanted to meet you first."

Soodabeh glanced over at Kaveh but he averted his eyes and turned his attention back to Kyan. "Do you know how to ride a horse?"

"No!" replied Kyan. "I live in Tehran. There's nothing there but smoke and dust."

"But the great Alborz Mountain surrounding it is magnificent." He went on after a brief pause. "Do you ever go skiing at Abali?"

"No, I honestly don't know much other than work."

Soodabeh piped in. "I met Kyan a while back at a seminar in Shiraz."

"Did you read Hafez divinations?"

Kyan smiled. *"The lost Yousef will return to Kanan; worry not..."*

"If only..." replied Kaveh.

His expression was serious. Soodabeh was puzzled as she watched him. He said nothing further, sat there quiet for a bit, drank from the glass of water on the table, the stared at the sky in silence. It seemed his mind was somewhere else. A few moments passed without a sound, then Kaveh rose and began to head out. "You'll have to forgive me; I'm extremely tired. I can't be a good companion for you. I'll try to get some rest now. Think of this place as your home; ask Moosa for anything you need. He'll take care of it for you."

After these words he went inside. Soodabeh was incredulous; she couldn't understand why he had so bluntly dismissed them. But Kyan could see Kaveh's love for Soodabeh written all over his face.

Soodabeh and Kyan left after an hour without Kaveh even saying goodbye to them. On the road she was quiet and downcast the entire time. "He's an interesting man," said Kyan. "He loves you very much as well."

"No! He loves someone else."

Kyan breathed a sigh of relief. "In that case, when should I bring my family for the marriage proposal?" She did not answer him; her mind was elsewhere. She wanted to go back to Kaveh. She was already missing him.

The next day, Soodabeh called Salar to check on Kaveh. "He wasn't himself yesterday."

"Don't worry," replied Salar. "He's alright. Just tell me the dates for your engagement and wedding."

"Who ever talked about engagement and marriage? We're just colleagues."

"But I've heard Kyan's madly in love with you... It's beyond just working together."

"Honestly, even I don't know what I want," Soodabeh confessed. "My mind is all over the place."

"Is one of those places America?" asked Salar.

"No, I've been free from that thought for a long time. The spell is lifted!"

He laughed. "I knew it."

Soodabeh had been unfocused and distracted for a while now, tormented by an odd feeling. The fear of losing Kaveh frightened her! She badly needed his companionship. A world without Kaveh was unthinkable. She struggled with her emotions for a few days, but finally relented and called him.

"He's gone to Mr. Erfan's house," said Moosa who answered the phone.

"Who is Mr. Erfan?"

"He's a wise man that Mr. Kaveh calls on whenever life gets difficult."

Soodabeh felt something was strange. Moosa added, "He's been rather stressed lately. It's not clear why he's so tense. I hope speaking with Mr. Erfan helps him feel better."

Soodabeh was beginning to sense that Kaveh is in the same emotional state as herself. She wondered if it was possible that her feelings for him were mutual. "Well, when he comes back, tell him to call me," she told Moosa before hanging up.

....

Soodabeh and Kyan went out to dinner a couple of times, but she wasn't a good companion. Her heart kept racing. She called Kaveh one more time. Moosa answered again.

"He's gone horseback riding. He'll be back late."

"Did you give him my message?"

"Yes, I did. But he didn't say anything."

Soodabeh was crushed. She tried to rationalize things to herself: "Why am I upset? So he doesn't want to call! He's got a lot to do... he didn't even contact his father for months at a time. He's just weird!"

But these excuses didn't satisfy her. Unpleasant thoughts wouldn't leave her alone. She was perplexed by her sentiments. A new passion had blossomed in her heart; not seeing Kaveh was agonizing. Auntie had observed the change in Soodabeh's temperament and noticed her agitation and reclusiveness. She called Salar. "I don't know what's ailing Soodabeh. She's not well at all."

"She's probably in love!" said Salar teasingly.

"In love with whom?" asked Auntie.

"She had brought Kyan over to meet Kaveh."

"Well, if Kyan is a good man she should marry him," Auntie thought out loud.

. . . .

Three months passed and Soodabeh was still in conflict with her emotions. Finally one day she phoned Salar.

"I don't know why Kaveh doesn't answer my calls. Has something happened?"

"He's quite busy... He's planning to go to America for a seminar on raising livestock."

Her heart sank. She paused and said, "Well, this one is leaving too."

"He's not going there to stay," answered Salar.

"You never know! They go and never come back!"

"Kaveh will come back. Everything and everyone he has is here."

"Like Farhad?!" asked Soodabeh sarcastically.

"My dear Soodabeh, have some compassion for Farhad," pleaded Salar. "Forgive him. Life dealt him such a blow that he won't recover any time soon."

"He should have known better," retorted Soodabeh. "He should have made the right decision.

"Believe me, it's my fault," insisted Salar. "When Goli died, I constantly pressured my children to pursue higher education; that's what he was chasing after. I'm the one at fault."

"No, Salar, you're not responsible. No one is. It's all his own doing. The difference between humans and animals is the right to choose; it just takes spiritual strength and willpower to make the right selection. People who've made a positive mark in human history were those who made the correct decisions; you told us this yourself. Isn't that true?"

"Yes, you're right," said Salar with resignation. "Now tell me have you made your choice?"

"I'm struggling day and night."

"So you haven't chosen yet!"

"No!"

"Thank God," exclaimed Salar. "When you do decide, come for a visit. I want to see you."

When their conversation ended, Soodabeh felt like she could finally breathe. Her mood had improved; her thoughts were focused and she knew what she wanted. She was surprised at her lack of insight up till now. She wished to share her sentiments with someone. She wished her father was there to talk to. Ahmad Ramzi had always managed to be in touch with his children, but they still tended to share their worries and dilemmas with Salar, even now that he no longer lived at the Ramzi house.

Soodabeh could not forget Salar's last question about her having made a choice. It kept flashing in her mind. She knew he had asked her a serious question and required a serious and clear answer. She also knew what that answer is; her true inclination was clear and there was no doubt. She now knew what to say in response to Kyan's proposal! She had to see him as soon as possible.

Two days after talking to Salar, Soodabeh showed up at Kyan's office without prior notice. He was surprised to see her at that time of day. Looking at her serious expression, his heart sank.

"I cannot marry you," said Soodabeh without preface. "I can't lie to you and base my life on fraud and deception. My heart belongs to someone else. I never knew how much I loved him until now, but I truly can't live without him. You have to forgive me!"

Color drained from Kyan's face. He sat behind his desk, looking dejectedly at Soodabeh. "I pray to God that Kaveh is worthy of a love like yours and a person like you."

She looked at him startled! How did he know her love is Kaveh?

....

From there, Soodabeh headed straight home. "I'm going to the farm," she told Auntie. "I have to see Kaveh." She then called Ahmad Ramzi. "Father! I'm going to the farm to be with Kaveh, do you want anything?"

"Kaveh is supposed to come to Tehran soon to obtain a visa for America," said her father. "Do you have something on your mind for going there?"

"I can't say it now. But I have to see him!"

She then drove to Isfahan.

Kaveh hadn't slept well the night before. Beat and tired, he told Moosa, "I'm not coming to the farm today... I'm exhausted. I'll stay here on the balcony and read a book."It was a spring day. The trees had blossomed and the farm had turned green all over. The scent of red roses and Jasmines filled the air, stroking Kaveh's senses.

"Where is your father?" asked Moosa.

"He's at my uncle's house and won't be back till dinnertime. Bring me some fruit."

"You won't eat lunch?"

"No, I'll just eat the fruit. That'll be enough."

Picking up his book, Kaveh sat on one of the lounge chairs, put his legs on the table, started reading and lost track of time. In the afternoon he heard a vehicle approaching. Then he saw Soodabeh's car stop in front of the building. His heart began fluttering! Soodabeh got out of the car, wearing a stylish orange manto and a green flower-patterned scarf which she took off her hair, allowing her shiny, jet black mane to dance in the wind. Her seductive brown eyes sparkled.

Kaveh had never seen her so alluring. Feeling butterflies in his stomach, he put his book down and stood up. "Welcome!" he said calmly yet enthusiastically. "You brought joy to our home. Come sit and rest."

Soodabeh sat next to him. "You're not answering my calls on purpose?" she asked. "Do you want to torment me?"

Kaveh looked at her puzzled. "Forgive me, I've been busy. I forgot."

Soodabeh became agitated. "You've been busy? Didn't even have time to answer a single phone call?"

"Well, I didn't know my phone calls are this important to you."

She was now genuinely angry. "You dragged me all the way here so I could fall at your feet, tell you I love you, I don't want to be away from you or live even for a moment without you. Is this what you wanted?"

Kaveh felt euphoric. He was brimming with joy and love inside. As they sat there, he took Soodabeh by the hand, pulled her over to him and kissed her lips passionately. "Well, I wanted you to decide on your own," he told her. "I couldn't make up your mind for you... Kyan is handsome, intelligent and talented, Farhad the complete package. But Kaveh is an ugly cripple with a hunched back... I couldn't be the one deciding. Now you get it?"

Soodabeh took his hand and placed it on her cheek. He held her again and whispered, "Now that it's turned out this way, will you marry me?"

She smiled, revealing two dimples on her cheeks that amplified her beauty and drove Kaveh senseless with desire. She then stood up. "You forced me to propose to you. Now you're asking if I'll marry you?"

He laughed. "Select the day as soon as possible."

"I'll talk to my father and set up a date."

"Have you seen the house I built for you?" asked Kaveh.

"Which one?"

"That big mansion at the end of the farm… How did you miss it?"

"You built that for me?" she asked joyfully. "When?"

"I designed it a few months back and it was finished last week. How can we expect our kids to live here in such a rundown building!"

"How did you know we would get married?"

"I knew it," answered Kaveh. "I just didn't know when!"

"Where is Salar?" she asked.

"He went to see my uncle. He'll be back for dinner."

"Then I should go make some food."

"You can't cook wearing this chic dress and those high heels," he told her jokingly. "Let's just sit and eat some fried eggs with bread and cheese."

It didn't take long for Salar to arrive. "Father, Soodabeh is here with good news…" exclaimed Kaveh. "We're planning to get married. Do you approve?"

Salar's face brightened up with a smile. "She finally made her choice!"

"We must have a grand wedding," said Kaveh to his father. "A ceremony so dazzling and glorious it will leave everyone in awe. Spend as much as you like, father. Illuminate the farm; light up torches; turn this place into a paradise."

He then turned to Soodabeh. "Put on some comfortable shoes and let's go. I want to show you your new house. And don't leave my side again."

He locked eyes passionately with Soodabeh. His gaze pierced through her soul like a shooting star, and she felt a rush of exhilaration.